"You ready to give lassoing a try?"

Gage walked over and unfastened the loop, recoiling the rope to its original position.

Willow shook her head and finally grabbed her writing instruments, taking a seat on the bench. "I want to write it all down so I can remember it later."

She opened her journal and began recording the images so vivid in her mind.

"Like I said, practice is the way to make yourself good at it." He turned around and built his loop again, throwing it a second time, only to miss.

She looked up from her scribbling. "Why did you miss?"

"The truth?"

"Always." She stared and wondered why he'd even considered being anything but honest with her.

"You distracted me."

She usually messed herself up and didn't mind taking the blame if she was truly guilty of causing trouble for someone else, but she'd been nowhere near his target. "How did I do that?"

Gage retrieved his rope and strolled over to sit beside her on the bench.

"I let you. I was paying more attention to your hair than I was the picket."

DeWanna Pace is a *New York Times* and *USA TODAY* bestselling author. She has published two dozen novels and anthologies, several of which have been chosen as book club selections by Doubleday, Rhapsody, Book-of-the-Month, *Woman's Day* and The Literary Guild. DeWanna combines her faith with her love of humor and historical romance. Let her show you the ways a heart can love.

Books by DeWanna Pace

Love Inspired Historical

The Daddy List
The Texas Ranger's Secret

DeWANNA PACE

The Texas Ranger's Secret

HARLEQUIN® LOVE INSPIRED® HISTORICAL

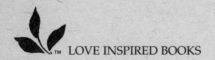

™ LOVE INSPIRED BOOKS

ISBN-13: 978-0-373-28344-6

The Texas Ranger's Secret

Copyright © 2016 by DeWanna Pace

And whatsoever ye do in word or deed,
do all in the name of the Lord Jesus,
giving thanks to God and the Father by Him.
—*Colossians* 3:17

Chapter One

May 1868

The thunderstorm rushed ahead of Willow McMurtry, as if warning all who lived in High Plains, Texas, that she would arrive and with her came trouble.

Seeking a new path because she couldn't stay on her last one, she prayed, *Please don't let me mess up in this town, too.*

Wind buffeted the curtain meant to keep out the dust stirred up beneath the churning hooves of the horses pulling the overland stage. Lightning bolts blinked in and out as the curtain flapped back and forth, offering popping whips of relief from the oppressive heat to the only passenger who had not yet reached her destination.

With glimpses of the passing prairie, she watched uprooted vegetation tumble toward the coach searching for a barrier to the wind's fury. But the team's pounding hooves and the coach's wheels crushed the wind-driven fodder or ricocheted it hither and yonder across the countryside.

"High Plains ahead!" yelled the driver, heralding the blessed fact that the long journey was near its end.

At least for now.

She would finally be inside somewhere, out of biting range of bugs and flies trying to hitch a ride.

"One-hour stop, coming up!"

The sense of stifling solitude gripped Willow even more profoundly, threatening to spill the unshed tears she'd held back when she'd said goodbye to the other passengers many miles ago. How she hated to be alone, and wanted so desperately to be among friends—a tribe of her own. A tribe made not just of family members, who were expected to include her, but friends who chose and enjoyed being in her company.

Willow called upon the light of hope living within her that this place so loved by her sisters might also prove the haven that would welcome her, rescue her from herself and become a home to her if she could not resolve her problem back in Georgia.

How much she wanted to be an asset to a community rather than an object of scorn. A blessing to someone, not a hindrance.

She took a lace kerchief from her reticule, then dabbed the perspiration dotting her face and neck, hoping to make herself look more presentable for when she arrived. Willow pinched her cheeks a little to add color, then brushed her fingers through wisps of hair that had gone astray from her upswept curls.

She put away her kerchief and lifted the emerald hat from her lap and did her best to nest it back in place at a jaunty angle. But her height in such a confined space gave little room to set it fashionably atop her head. The seat kept rocking and swaying to the point she finally just had to jab the hat pin in and hope for the best.

The plumed ostrich feather adorning the hat hung too far over her left eye, bent out of shape by the last woman who'd left the coach in Fort Worth. She'd accidentally stumbled over Willow's long legs and ended up plopping down on one edge of the hat. Her apology had sounded so sincere that Willow hadn't had the heart to complain. After all, she wasn't exactly graceful herself most of the time and hoped others would forgive her lack of coordination.

Sighing in frustration, she decided it certainly wouldn't be the first time she arrived somewhere looking disheveled. Daisy and Snow wouldn't be surprised at all, but Willow had wanted to make a good impression on her future brother-in-law and anyone else who came with her sisters to fetch her.

She did her utmost to adjust the hat but only ended up making the feather look more like quilt padding dangling from a fishing line and her head feel like a pincushion. Maybe she'd have time to dig into her baggage and take a brush to her mop of hair and just go hatless, but the mighty winds that swept the Texas prairie almost required a soul to wear some kind of bonnet or head covering. Unless she chose to braid her hair, as Daisy always did.

She couldn't wait to see her sisters. Daisy's impending wedding had come as a surprise and provided a most convenient excuse for quick departure from Atlanta.

When Willow told her boss that Daisy needed her to help take care of the children while the couple honeymooned, he had eagerly agreed that her absence just might prove the perfect solution to the trouble she'd caused.

Willow had left, unsure if she would ever return to her job at the paper but knowing this leave might be the only way to improve her chances of being asked back.

Not only that, she felt that she really had to be there for Daisy and Snow. Willow only hoped she hadn't arrived too late to attend the wedding and be of some help. Daisy would never say a word, of course, but her middle sister rarely held anything back from Willow. Now she and Snow would be spending two months together without the buffer of their older sister.

The thought made Willow pray once more that she somehow arrived on time.

"Whoa, you beastly beauties! Hold up there, now," shouted the driver as his last pull on the reins brought the team to a halt.

Willow pitched forward into the seat across from hers. She dug in the heels of her kid boots and grabbed the side of the coach in an effort to reseat herself, only to slide bottom-first to the floor. Her hat shifted. The feather dipped low to tickle her nose, which set off a round of sneezing made worse by the billowing dust as the stagecoach settled.

She stretched out her arms to see if she could leverage herself enough to climb the walls and regain her seat, but to no avail. She'd just have to sit there like a folded accordion and scoot out the door once the driver opened it.

"Safe and delivered," yelled the coachman. "Only half past noon."

Half past noon? They'd been due in more than two and a half hours ago. One of the wheels had hit a rut and taken quite a while to be repaired. Her sisters would be madder than two snakes with no rattles thinking she'd missed the stage that would get her here in time for the ceremony.

Willow knew Daisy had been meeting several stages the past two months. Her sister had a right to be angry with her for not showing up. When Daisy invited her and Snow for a visit in March, Snow had gone on alone. Willow had promised to come later, wanting to arrive with a wonderful announcement of her own—a job at the respected newspaper in Atlanta.

Why hadn't she just gone to High Plains when she first promised?

Because I wanted to prove to everybody how capable I am, she berated herself as she struggled again to dislodge her body. *Now look at me. I can't even untangle my legs.*

At twenty-two, she was beginning to believe she'd never find a place where she could be proud of herself and find what she could do well.

She should have never risked taking the position as printer's helper at the *Weekly Chronicle*, knowing she'd promised Daisy the visit.

If only her boss hadn't mentioned his love of anything Texas that first day of work, she might have kept her mouth shut.

But no, she couldn't wait to share some of her late grandfather's tales of his legendary days riding with Captain Jack Hays, one of the bravest captains in the Texas Corps of Rangers.

That was just the start of her troubles. If only she'd been aware of what she'd stirred up at the time. Then again, she never recognized the exact moment she set herself up for failure. Did anyone?

What was taking the driver so long? She didn't have that much baggage. Surely he would let her out first before changing the team.

Her legs cramped but she didn't want to seem impatient with the man. After all, he wasn't aware that she'd jammed herself between the seats. She'd just have to sit here and keep her mind on something until he opened the coach door and rescued her.

Willow's thoughts returned to the days that followed her boss's unusual interest in learning more of Texas. She'd told him of how her grandfather had read to her and her siblings the eight-page newspaper serials called story papers and that she'd preferred the frontier tales of derring-do about adventurous heroes.

She spouted a wealth of the jargon, giving him lots of details regarding the lifestyle and ways of the men who worked the ranging companies, feeling proud she recalled so much after all these years.

Biven Wittenburg Harrington III decided to take a risk and develop a limited series of story papers based on a fictional Texas Ranger and see how well the readers responded. Literacy was up and her boss-editor-publisher said he believed readers yearned for something to take their minds off the hard news of Reconstruction.

When he turned to her, Willow first realized she might be headed for more trouble than she knew how to handle.

He asked her to write the fictional stories under the name Will Ketchum, based on her grandfather's tales. She should have listened to her initial hesitation, but she was being offered the biggest blessing of a would-be writer's lifetime. A chance to reach readers.

Willow asked herself if she was ready for her dream. Was she capable of meeting such a challenge? The only way she would find out was to put aside her hesitation and do her best.

But her best proved as frustrating as pinning her hat back on today. Critics railed her efforts as pure fiction with no foundation in truth. Though the stories were never presented as anything but fable, the "no foundation in truth" complaint hurt her feelings. She had besmirched her grandfather's memory and failed her boss's expectations.

After researching further, she discovered Grandfather had taken creative license and jumbled parts of the facts. She even learned that a few of the stories he'd told hadn't happened until after he'd retired from life as a Ranger and moved to Grandmother's hometown in Florida. The criticism about lacking believability proved justified.

She understood now where she'd inherited some of her traits.

Surprisingly, when she went to Biven about what she'd discovered, he assured her that he expected the more conservative critics to berate any fiction he included in the paper, but it was clear from other readers' letters that they wanted equal parts fact and fiction in the serial. He'd decided on a delay in future stories about Ketchum until she could improve that balance.

Exhaling a huge sigh, Willow hoped High Plains would provide the solutions needed to set things right with his expectations…or at least offer a hideout from anyone learning she had authored the tales that had stirred up so much gossip.

She probably wouldn't have to worry about either if they found her all shriveled up between the coach seats.

"About ready to get out of there, miss?"

No, I enjoy my knees poking me in the chin, she thought, but called upon the only gracious bone left in her body when she hollered instead, "Yes, please. I need help down, if you don't mind."

The coach door swung wide and the driver's darkly stained leather glove thrust inside, offering a hand. "Problem?"

"I'm kind of stuck." Willow inched her slender frame toward him, finally managing to scoot sideways enough to twist her legs without shifting her crinoline petticoats too high. *Use his language*, she reminded herself. "Thank you, partner. I'm much obliged."

"Better hurry—you'll want to get inside somewhere," he warned. "Looks like it's fixing to drop buckets out here."

"How 'bout I help? You take care of getting her bags down," offered a deeply masculine voice. "Then we'll both change out the team."

What *had* they been doing? Discussing the weather?

A hand twice as big as the driver's reached in and latched on to Willow's forearm, giving a mighty jerk that unfolded her.

"Thank y—" Her breath escaped as momentum carried Willow out, one of her boots skidding off the first step down, the other meeting only air.

Out she tumbled, tripping on the step, only to land face-first into the broad chest of a massive-sized man and knock him flat on his back.

He roared with laughter and batted away the

feather sprawled on his face. "Welcome to High Plains, lady. Glad to meetcha."

"Oh, do pardon me, partner." Her lashes blinked rapidly, trying to widen her dust-filled eyes enough to see clearly.

"Bear. The name's Bear. Blacksmith and livery-man." Amusement shone in his brown eyes as he waited for her to stand. "And I figure that was most of my doing. My wife says I don't know my own strength sometimes."

The bald man stood and handed Willow her hat, an apologetic expression slanting his lips to one side. "Guess I'm gonna have to buy ya a new one, miss. That bird looks plenty plucked."

She accepted her hat and shook her head. "No need, Mr., uh…" She realized she didn't know if the name he'd given was his first or last. "Bear. The hat was already ruined before I got out of the coach." She launched into a brief explanation.

"Anybody else in there?" He looked past her.

"No, I'm the only one left," she informed, wondering if he'd deliberately cut her explanation short.

"Well, then is there anything else I can do for ya since I handled ya too rough?"

Willow glanced around the immediate vicinity, taking note of the people milling on the sidewalks, a couple of vendors hawking their wares, a wagon parked in front of what she thought she remembered was a mercantile. She hadn't been here since she was fourteen years old, when her niece was born. She'd not really paid that much attention to the town at the time. Boys were too much her focus back then. Willow supposed that was where she'd gotten her imaginings of what Will Ketchum might look and sound like. Texas males had a swagger about them and an interesting accent.

"Can you tell me if Daisy Trumbo or Snow McMurtry have been here today asking for me?" she finally inquired. "I'm their sister, and they were supposed to meet my stage."

Bear walked to the back of the coach and took the baggage the driver lifted down, then set the mail sacks closer to his quarters. "So you're the one," he said. "Come to think of it, you kind of look like them, and they said you'd probably arrive without a bonnet."

Did she have to be so predictable? And what did he mean when he said, "So you're the one"? "Then they've been here and gone?"

"Told me they still had too much to do for the wedding tomorrow to stick around for a late stage. Some never arrived at all and several you've missed, according to Tadpole. Oh, sorry, that's what I call your niece, Ollie. She's my fishing partner. Guess you can understand the sense of their thinking."

Relief and frustration washed through Willow as she brushed back her hair. She hadn't missed the wedding as she'd feared but the man knew from dealing with stage arrivals and her niece that Daisy had expected her long before now. Some first impression she'd made on Bear.

"I'm supposed to tell ya they'll check back around three to see if the stage made it or not."

They meant if I made it or not. Willow wished she didn't always disappoint them. That was something she really meant to work on while she was here. Though both loved her deeply, she wanted them to be proud of her, to see that she could improve and to have faith in her when it counted most. She didn't want to fail them or herself anymore.

Willow exhaled a long breath, setting her shoulders to the two-and-a-half-hour wait, wishing that was all the time it would take to improve herself and give her an idea how best to get started learning fact from fiction. She'd considered different ways to go about satisfying her editor's request in the time she'd be here watching the children. After all, who knew better about Texas than Texans?

Bear took her baggage to the livery and set it just inside the door. "We'll keep these here until your sisters turn up. You can go about your business for a while and your bags will be waiting for ya."

When she didn't move, he motioned to his quarters next to the livery. "My wife's taken ill or I'd invite ya in. Are you a Miss McMurtry or a Mrs. Somebody?"

She realized she hadn't given him her name. "Miss Willow McMurtry. I'm the youngest of the three."

"If you'll give me some time to help Gus get the team changed and the stage on its way, Miss Mc-Murtry, I'll see what I can do about getting ya some tea." He motioned across the road. "Of course, you could always wait over at the diner. I can let your sisters know where you are when I see them. You must be hungrier than a polecat if you've been traveling all morning."

Though she would have loved to go inside, Willow shook her head, which served only to loosen her top knot of curls. "Not hungry at all, and I don't want to put you to any trouble, especially with your wife sick. I'll wait until I'm at Daisy's."

The last thing she wanted was to make her first public appearance in a crowd looking this side of insane. It was embarrassing enough that Bear had seen her this way. Visiting the diner was out of the question. "Mind if I just wait out here?"

She explained that she wanted to put her best foot forward, so to speak. Even though she hadn't, in fact.

"No problem." Bear glanced up at the overhanging clouds and started backing up. "I've got to get that mail in and sorted before it gets wet. Feel free to take shelter inside the livery. I always keep a couple of fresh blankets on the shelf, if ya get chilled. There's a lantern or a stove, if you need it. Like I said, I'll let the ladies know you're here if they don't spot ya right off."

"I appreciate it, and I hope I get to meet Mrs. Bear when she's..." Willow could tell he was eager to be about his business. She'd learned that people tended to back up from her when she kept prattling and they really wanted to be on their way.

The driver said something to the smithy and Bear took the opportunity to dash away to grab the mailbags.

Maybe she ought to make a list of all the don't-dos she needed to remember. *One: don't get too chatty,* she chastised herself, *even if the Texan is chatty himself.* She'd always been told Texans were known to be the strong silent types. She'd have to revise that old belief. They liked their women less talkative than themselves.

Her eyes focused on the town again, and she thought it might be best to take this time to familiarize herself with what she remembered about High Plains. She didn't want to leave the livery yard. That way her sisters could easily spot her, and she preferred not to be by herself in the livery. She hated being alone. At least out here, she could watch people milling around.

It was then she saw him.

A dark-haired stranger standing in the alley between the boarding house and the mercantile, leaning against one of the outer walls. Tall and lean, he wore a long black duster that hung to the top of his spurs, and his boots stretched clear to his knees. The duster was pulled back over a pistol-filled holster that rode low on his right thigh. His right hand remained gloveless, making anyone aware he was proficient at shooting from that side. Her gaze swept past his broad chest, and she noted he favored a scruff of a beard and mustache. A hat shaded his eyes. Though she couldn't determine their color, the force of their intensity touched her even this far away as she sensed him staring at her.

A chill of recognition ran up her spine, yet she'd never met the man. A handsome stranger who'd suddenly stepped out of her imagination? A hero? A villain?

Whoever he was, he looked exactly as she'd pictured Will Ketchum in her mind. Like the kind of man who would have ridden with her grandfather in his days of ranging. Her fictional character had sprung to life as a flesh-and-blood man right in front of her.

Would he talk like Ketchum?

If the stranger proved to be on the right side of the law, he just might be an answer to her prayer.

She started pacing, wondering how she could gain a proper introduction to him. Maybe she needed to practice saying "howdy" a little better.

The stage had come and gone. Still, the slender reddish-blond-haired woman remained in front of the livery talking to herself. Gage Newcomb thumbed up his hat brim and admired her persistence, if nothing else. How long would she wait for whoever was supposed to have met her there?

He'd made it his business to check out and make himself familiar with every new male or female who landed in High Plains these past few weeks, learning early on that Stanton Hodge knew no remorse in enlisting anyone to help him escape the long arm of justice. Lady, gent or fresh-out-of-short-britches lad could be party to Hodge's plans, so it wouldn't surprise Gage at all if this shapely newcomer had come to town to lend the outlaw aid.

But Hodge hadn't shown yet. Maybe the sidewinder was waiting for the weather to blow over.

Wherever the elusive horse thief might be holed up at this point, Gage meant to find him and turn him in or die trying. After that, he'd ride off into the Davis Mountains downstate and live his life alone, far away from so-called civilization. Far away from pity. Far enough to make sure he became a burden to no one.

That was the only way he could deal with accepting a future he'd wish on no soul.

He had tracked his longtime adversary here, ready to put an end to their six-month cat-and-mouse game before he gave his notice that this was his last manhunt as a Texas Ranger. He'd always brought in his man before. He didn't plan to fail his captain this time either.

Hodge had managed to stay out of sight so far. Gage suspected the viper was playing it slippery until things settled down from the recent bank robbery and town-burning attempt that were so fresh in everybody's mind here in High Plains. The thief probably wished he'd headed some other direction when he found out about the recent crime spree.

Hodge liked rattling about his feats and the wait to pull his next theft must have been eating at his ego.

That was the one thing Gage could count on. Lack of bragging rights would lure Hodge from his snake den to make a quick strike before things got too dull. Gage knew that was when he'd catch him off guard. The outlaw had been curled up and cozy too long now. Gage sensed the man would be getting anxious, and the woman pacing across the street might just be the pretty twist of petticoat Hodge would use to carry out his next crime.

He sure hoped not, but she wouldn't be the first woman he'd had to lock up.

As a man who saw the world as dark and the people in it as ready to do whatever they could to get away with something, Gage rarely gave the benefit of the doubt. He'd learned the hard way that a woman could be just as nefarious as any man.

But a man was his focus now. Gage rubbed the scars beneath and around his eyes, feeling the raised flesh and vowing vengeance once more upon the man whose actions were forcing him to choose a new way of life for himself. Being a Ranger was everything to Gage. If he lost that, he would be nothing. His failing eyesight would take his soul, his heart, his whole life. If a man looked weak, he'd forever bow down to others. Gage couldn't bear the thought of losing his whole identity.

Stanton Hodge had stolen something far more precious than the horses Gage was tracking him for.

He pushed aside his self-pity, and despite the clouded day and the threat of rain echoing in the thunder that rumbled above, he squinted hard to define this new arrival's approximate age.

Long years of riding saddle all over Texas made distances seem farther than they appeared, but she couldn't have been more than forty or fifty feet from where he stood. Still, he couldn't quite catch the color of her eyes or whether she had freckles. All he noted was that she was in her late teens or early twenties, and she had stealth to her walk, which revealed a long stretch of legs and decent health.

Maybe she would prove the break he was looking for in the case. Hodge often chose a young, impressionable gal able to travel fast.

Gage decided he'd watch her, find out her identity and make sure she was not sister, sweetheart or any other connection whatsoever to the man he would bring to justice.

The wind got up again, wailing through the alley and buffeting him hard enough that he had to rock back and forth on his spurs to catch his balance. A quick glance at the pretty lady revealed she fought the gale, as well, swatting down her billowing skirt.

A loud crack of thunder echoed across the sky. Then within seconds, large pellets of rain splattered the ground, leaving rows of golden eagle–sized dots. Grayish-yellow clouds dipped so low he could almost touch them, signaling their weight would not be contained any longer. High Plains was about to receive an onslaught of hard, pounding rain that would become a gully washer by the time it ended. Best to seek shelter until the Texas sky finished its tantrum.

Most folks took heed and headed inside the closest door available. Not the newcomer. She put her hat back on and glanced up at the sky, swiping at the dangling feather as if it were a pesky fly biting her. The wind suddenly spun her around so fast she fell to her knees. Gage bolted toward her to help, but she jumped to her feet and shook the dust from her skirt.

The steam of her anger seemed to radiate across the thoroughfare as the downpour came, soaking her from hem to haphazard hat.

The bull of a blacksmith ran out of his quarters and spoke to the woman. Gage halted in his tracks, waiting to see what she would do. The smithy pointed to his home, but she shook her head and elected to disappear inside the livery instead.

Gage's curiosity got the better of him as he watched the blacksmith dash home. Feather Hat's stubbornness made him wonder why she refused the better place to wait out the rain. He'd met Bear and his wife not long ago. Both were kind people who seemed to be well liked by everyone. That meant Feather Hat wasn't from around here. She was a stranger who didn't know them well enough to trust their hospitality. All the more reason to find out her identity and connection to Hodge, if any.

Soaked to his boot tops, Gage took off at a dead run for the livery. If she questioned his presence there, he would just tell her that he'd taken shelter in the nearest place he could find. That should allow at least some polite conversation between them and maybe he might learn a few things about her.

He stepped out of the rain and shook water from his duster, then tilted his hat to empty its brim. The sound of a match being struck against wood flared his nostrils as the pungent odor of sulfur and hissing kerosene filled the air.

"Ouch, that hurt!" exclaimed a female voice, then, "Oops! No! Oh, please, no, not that!"

Instinct made Gage look for a stove or a lantern, but reality flared in front of him as flames crept up one of the stall walls.

She had dropped the match.

A low, angry voice cut the air like a whip. "See if there's water in any of those buckets. Hurry!"

Willow heard the man's command before she saw him. He didn't sound like Bear. Not taking time to look at him or wonder who he was, she did as instructed and ran into the first stall ahead of her. Sure enough, one of the water buckets remained half-full.

"Here's one." She thrust the pail toward him and assumed he would take it.

"Throw what you've got over the flames and grab another," he ordered. "I'll beat out what I can with this."

She heard him beating something against the wall and, with a quick glance backward, realized where he'd come from. He'd taken off the trail coat she'd noticed earlier when she studied him in the alley.

Will Ketchum to the rescue, she thought, wishing this stranger could be the man she dreamed might someday come true.

"I—I broke my nail when I struck the match against the board." She shook her forefinger, embarrassed that such a small pain had caused all this. "It made me drop the match."

Horses whinnied in their stalls, their powerful legs dancing to get away from the threat that sent gray vapor spiraling into the air.

The stranger kept beating his coat against the wall. Orders fired in rapid succession. "Find another bucket, lady. Be careful. Don't go near the horses. They'll stomp you to death. Got to get this out before it reaches the loft. That hay goes up, we'll all go up with it." One glance in her direction told her he wasn't worried about the finger she still held up.

She hurried, only to find nothing in the next three stalls. All that remained were the feed tins with the horses. Thunder roared overhead and a crack of lightning rent the air, telling her that it had struck close by.

Please, Lord. Don't let this happen to me. Don't let me burn down the livery on the first day here. And while it's raining, at that. If You're going to let it rain, let it be enough to put this out, please.

"There's no more. What do I do?" She searched for the blankets Bear had said were stored somewhere and found them on a shelf above where her baggage had been set.

Why hadn't she just grabbed one of them to keep warm instead of trying to light a lantern so she could see to make a proper fire in the potbellied stove?

She'd made a fire, all right.

Willow grabbed a blanket and shook it open to help him beat out the flames. A daddy longlegs spider ran across her hand. She screamed in fear.

The man raced toward her, swatted the spider away and exchanged his now-charred coat for the blanket.

"That kind of spider isn't poisonous even if it bites you," he assured her as he ran back and attacked the flames even harder.

The fire seemed to be climbing faster.

"Take empty buckets," he insisted. "The trough is outside closer to the blacksmith's quarters. Bring back what you can carry without spilling. Fast as you can. And don't worry about your nails."

Nails were the last things on her mind. Being burned or bitten occupied her every thought. She grabbed the pails and ran, determined to carry both back full and in time. She spotted the trough quickly and the first bucket wasn't that hard to fill. The second proved almost unmanageable once she was done and tried to lift both.

With every step, the water sloshed over the sides until she had to take slower ones to keep from spilling it. Her pulse raced, thrumming in her ears, lodging in her throat in a dry knot that felt as if it were drumming to her heartbeat.

As she finally reached the livery, she had to set a bucket down to open the door but forgot to move it back far enough to allow her enough space to enter. *Not now*, she prayed. *Please let me prove helpful. I've got to save him. The horses, too.*

What to do? What to do? Willow took one boot and scooted the bucket backward. It inched away. Another scoot. Too hard this time. The bucket tilted.

"No, don't spill!" She couldn't keep her prayer silent. Her boot hurried to sweep around the pail to prevent it from turning over. She misjudged the distance and ended up stepping directly into the tin container, sloshing water everywhere.

Willow grabbed the door and jerked it backward as she removed her foot from the almost empty bucket. One would just have to do for now.

She gathered the remaining pail in hand and ran toward the cowboy, relieved to see his battle with the fire had taken a turn for the better.

He emptied a bucket on the flames.

Where had he gotten that from? One of the horse stalls? How brave!

"Move out of the way," she shouted, wanting to let him rest a moment while she took over. It was the least she could do.

Instead of stepping aside as she threw the water from her pail, he turned.

A faceful of her helpfulness drenched him just

before the liquid hit its true mark, extinguishing the threat of fire.

"Oh, my," she said, dropping the pail as her hands shot to her mouth. "I didn't mean to do that, mister. Honestly. The bucket was so heavy and you didn't… I mean… I guess my aim was off."

He sputtered and tipped the brim of his hat so the water could run off. Before he settled it back on his head, he wiped his eyes with his forearm and blinked hard. "Actually, your aim was perfect, pretty lady. Your timing stinks. You could use a little improvement there."

His admonishment hit her right where she hurt most—her past. Her need of a better future. But she heard the truth in his criticism. Timing was everything. It might just be the one skill she needed to learn in order to improve all the others she wanted to handle better.

After all, learning to do everything right the first time would sure make everything easier and save her lots of embarrassment.

Question was, she wondered as a possibility sparked in her mind, did he have the necessary skills to teach her what she needed to learn—and would he even want to?

Looking up into his warm eyes, she thought for a blink she saw laughter. Would he be someone who'd help? Someone who'd understand? Or someone who'd judge?

Chapter Two

The barn burner grabbed another blanket off the shelf and carefully fanned it out, he supposed to make sure no more critters had set up house among the folds. She approached Gage as if she meant to cover him with it.

"Here, let me help you dry," she offered.

He allowed her close enough to smell the hint of some flower that had wilted and lost part of its fragrance. Peach blossoms, maybe. Dying on the vine. Probably the effect of the long stage ride on whatever perfume she wore mixed with her sodden clothing. Sweat didn't smell any prettier on a woman than it did on a man.

Gage waved away her effort, not wanting the blanket's coarse material anywhere near his face. After six months of suffering from the tender flesh beneath his eyes and not being able to wear a bandanna over his nose all winter, he avoided anything getting close enough to cause further pain. "I'm fine. Keep the blanket for yourself. You're wetter than I am. You didn't get that much on me."

"I'm sorry. I didn't mean to soak you." Feather Hat looked genuinely apologetic.

"Won't be the first time I got water thrown in my face. Besides, I was still wet from the rain."

"I'll make it up to you, sir." She wrapped the fresh blanket around her. "Just as I plan to replace the wood for Mr. Bear."

"Just Bear." Gage gathered the pails and returned all but one to the stalls. The horses were calming down now that the fire was out and the haze of smoke moved higher into the rafters. "Bear and his wife, Pigeon, prefer you call them by their first names. The Funderburgs probably won't let you repay them for the damage or they'll make it easy for you to repair it. They're good people."

"Good people deserve respect, too." Her gaze swept to the charred wall. "I'll make it up to them. I'll figure out some way."

He didn't know her from seed to high cotton, but the determination in her eyes impressed him. She meant business. Bear was about to get himself a new livery wall. Maybe he could lend a hand in helping her fix it.

She seemed to be waiting for him to speak or do something and Gage wasn't sure what. He'd been so focused on determining her odd eye color, unsure if his eyes were playing tricks on him or if this really was her true shade. Not quite honey colored, but like brand-new buckskin. Palomino pretty. Something he was glad to have a chance to see before he no longer could.

Gage decided to clean up the mess for Bear and maybe that would give him and the lady some time to get to know each other a bit before she had to go. When he took a pitchfork and raked some of the ashes into the last pail he hadn't returned, she tried to help by holding the pail steady and managed only to streak her cheeks and hands with soot.

She was about the most interesting woman he'd seen in a long time. Crazy hat and tangled hair, eyes the color of his favorite kind of horse and a smell that could make a man want to stand upwind of her. This woman made some kind of first impression.

He guessed he was like other men, favoring a pretty filly who kept up with her appearance and made him proud to walk beside her, but he didn't care for fussy women who took preening too far and ate up a man's time with vanity.

As intrigued as he was by her, he needed to make sure he remembered his primary goal—to learn if she was strong willed on the inside or easily coerced.

Feather Hat had been watching him expectantly, and finally she unwrapped the blanket and spread it over a squared-off bale of straw, then sat. After clearing her throat, she asked, "And you are?"

So that was what she'd been waiting on. His name.

Not one to apologize for anything, Gage merely said, "Newcomb."

She waited longer, then finally asked, "First or last name?"

"Last."

"You Texans don't talk much, do you?" She eyed him from head to toe.

Check that question off his list about her. She hailed from another state. "Not much except when there's something big to say. You from back east?"

"Occasionally." She shrugged her shoulders.

That got his attention. What was that supposed to mean? She either was or wasn't. "You care to be more specific?"

"I grew up in Florida, but I tend to move around a lot. I've lived north, east, visited the Deep South, Georgia, and now here I am in the West, though I haven't gotten any farther than Texas yet. Have you been here long?"

He wouldn't tell her much, just enough to make her feel more comfortable in revealing details about herself. "Been in town for about six weeks now. It's got a lot to offer if you're looking for a place to settle. You plan on sticking around or will you be moving on soon since it's clear you like to wander?"

"I'm here for my sister's wedding. She's getting married tomorrow."

"Oh, so you're the one." That explained a lot and helped set aside some of his suspicion about any connection she might have to Hodge. Still, she was the perfect type for his foe to enlist. Better keep watch over her while she stayed. Wouldn't want her making the wrong kind of friend and not being able to leave when and if she wanted to.

She stood, her fists knotting at her hips. "Does everyone in this town know I'm late?"

"Most everyone, near as I can tell. You're the source of a good many wagers over at the Twisted Spur anytime the stage is due in. They'll be mighty disappointed to see you've finally arrived. You've made some of the fellas a pretty penny this spring."

"The Twisted Spur?"

"The saloon."

"Just wonderful." Her fists unknotted and her palms flung upward. "I'm already the subject of gossip and I haven't even been here a few hours. I'll never make friends with anybody in the ladies' society, that's for sure."

Insecurity echoed behind her anger. She wanted people to think kindly of her. From the way she talked, Gage slightly altered his first estimation of her. This woman wasn't the sort that would easily take up with Hodge. She probably wouldn't even visit anywhere the thief normally caroused. Still, Hodge wouldn't let that stop him if he took notice of her and decided to make her a target or an accomplice. Stanton Hodge didn't care what others thought of him or whom he hurt.

Protective instincts stirred in Gage and he added one more goal to his last manhunt. If she proved as innocent as she appeared, he would make sure the man he tracked did not lure her into his conniving ways.

"Speaking of friends, when will your sisters come after you?" Gage had expected she would have been picked up by now.

Her palms fell back to her side. "Bear said around three o'clock. That should be anytime now, don't you think? I can go check outside. I noticed a clock on the water tower behind the livery."

She headed to the door but halted when Gage's words stopped her. "No need. They'll probably show up after the rain stops. Might as well keep dry as you can. I'll go ahead and light the lantern. You warm enough or you need the stove heated?"

"I've had enough fire for one day myself, but if you're cold, suit yourself. You'll probably do a better job of getting it going than I did."

She sounded defeated. Something buried long ago that he hadn't allowed himself to dig up since he was eleven years old twisted inside him. The last thing his father had ever teased him about was having gangly legs and broomstick arms, being a late bloomer.

That day, he'd been expected to watch for signs of the lobo attacking their herd. Gage had tired from his duty and started daydreaming, writing poetry in his thoughts, losing track of time. Next thing he knew, his father screamed at him to shoot to kill. Two cows were down, his father's leg caught and bleeding profusely in one of the traps set for the wolf. Champion tumbled in a vicious battle with the lobo, the dog's and the wolf's snarls jerking Gage to his feet.

All of a sudden, a high-pitched yelp tore from Champion's throat and he fell backward. The lobo had taken the last breath from the dog's body.

Gage's broomstick arms could hardly lift that big old rifle back then, but he vowed to stop the wolf from turning on his father. He kept that vow and his gangly legs and arms managed to get his father home and his dog buried. Two weeks later, he'd buried his father beside his dog. From that day since, he'd never allowed another soul to see any sign of weakness within him.

He couldn't allow Feather Hat to feel defeated. There was always strength to be learned just from trying. From believing you could do something.

"You did all right." Not being around much of anyone but criminals, Gage didn't give compliments easily. "Maybe next time keep your nails clipped shorter."

She stared at her fingertips. "I'll take that under consideration."

Gage laughed. "Is that a fancy way of telling me to mind my own business?"

"Quick study, aren't you?"

"When I need to be," he answered, noting the challenge that sparked in those Palomino eyes. He liked that kind of sass.

"You must have a lot of skills at your disposal," she announced.

If her eyes had been pitchforks, they'd have been raking him from hat to spur.

She must be trying to use one of her better skills on him now. Gage noticed that she suddenly appeared a lot prettier than a few minutes ago, or else the smoke was clearing enough to let him see her much better. Maybe it was just the amber glow of the lantern light causing her to look all soft and her hair to look fluffed up a bit. Her skin could have been carved from a pearl-colored tusk of ivory he'd once seen on a ship in Galveston.

No matter how she'd managed to make herself more attractive, she still didn't smell any better.

"I've got a few skills," he admitted, deciding he'd let his mind wander way too much on the subject of what he could see of her. "Which one appeals to you most?"

"What if I said all of them?"

Suspicion blazed inside Gage like a fire that had been kindling below the surface and suddenly flared. Maybe she wasn't as innocent as he'd first believed. In his wondering about her identity, he'd never considered she might already know plenty about him. Who had told her? Hodge? "Why would you want to know what I can do?"

"I'd like to make you a proposition, Mr. Newcomb."

"You don't even know me."

"True, but you look like a man who knows how to handle himself well. You certainly showed me how to put out a fire."

"Desperation goes a long way in making a man think fast on his feet."

"It also goes a long way in making a woman think she's found the right man to teach her a few things. I'm willing to take a chance that what I need to learn could be learned from you, and I'm willing to pay you to teach me. I have a few questions I'd like to ask, if you can spare the time."

He had no time to spare for anything but his pursuit of Hodge. "You've got me till the rain stops. So shoot."

"That's exactly one of the questions I have." Willow had been uncertain how to proceed with her curiosity about Mr. Newcomb without his suspecting anything. She needed to learn any of his skills, his ways of thinking, how he interacted with people and why, all without disclosing anything about her pseudonym. "Can you teach me how to shoot, ride, lasso a stump and a few other Texas specialties?"

Her boss was willing to give her a chance to straighten out the mess if she could make Will Ketchum believable. She wanted to prove she could. Maybe getting this Newcomb fellow to teach her some things would prove the answer to her dilemma.

"Any Texan worth his salt can teach you those kinds of things. Even your sisters could. Why me?"

Newcomb thumbed back his hat and it was then that she finally got a good look at his eyes. A knot twisted in her stomach as she tried not to stare, but she knew he heard her gasp.

"Go ahead. Get it out of your system." He pulled off his hat and stared back at her, challenging her to peer closer. "It took me some getting used to myself."

"What happened?" She wished she weren't so curious, but the fact that he encouraged her to study his face helped her examine it more closely. A thick forest of dark lashes sheltered eyes the color of midnight with a touch of amethyst in their depths. They were so startling that the raw red welts spotting his face beneath and around each of them seemed a rude cruelty to mar his once-handsome features.

She wanted to smooth away the welts, say a prayer over each and ask God to be merciful and remove them. But when her hand reached up impulsively, he took a step backward. She had gone too far. Her desire to help always made her make a wrong move.

"Please tell me what happened," she repeated, her eyes moistening with sympathy. Clearly this was an injury he'd suffered not that long ago. Some of the skin had healed, but not all. What kind of man was he that he could suffer such a tragedy and still go about his business as if nothing were amiss? He was truly braver than most she'd ever met. What had he called it, a "Texan worth his salt"?

"Don't do that." His voice came gruff, his gaze targeting hers so quick that if it could have shot bullets, she'd have been stone-cold dead. "I won't be pitied."

He sure was touchy. She preferred a man who had a pleasant nature and was not so quick to show his temper. That was, she would if she ever decided to spend time with another one for courting purposes.

"That was the last thing I was thinking," she countered. "Maybe astonishment that you weren't afraid to show me. Certainly admiration for your being courageous enough to deal with the scars as if they didn't take a smidgen of handsomeness away from you."

"So you think I'm handsome." He lost his somber expression long enough to allow a quirk of a smile.

Willow thought that if she hadn't needed Newcomb so badly to help with research, she might have slapped his arrogant face. After all, he hadn't properly introduced himself. She still didn't know his first name, and now he was flirting with her.

He certainly didn't lack any confidence. She could use that characteristic to make him more believable as a Ranger. Rangers were known as men who lived by their own codes. As a reader, she found a confident hero easier to admire. Confident, not arrogant or egotistical. There was a fine difference.

"Yes," she conceded. "You're handsome and unafraid. You've got skills and you don't mind being honest with me. We just need to decide on a schedule that'll work for both of us."

"Let's get this straight." He settled his hat back on his head. "You're hiring me for something, which you haven't yet told me what for. It's not a problem that I'm only kind of handsome, and I'm supposed to teach you a set of skills, one of which is shooting. Does that about sum it up?"

She gave him a thumbs-up. "We understand each other perfectly."

"Like I said before, your sisters could teach you everything."

Willow shook her head. "I want a man's perspective. To make it believ— To learn it the way a man knows how." She'd almost slipped up.

"I'll have to think about this," he told her frankly.

"Willow!" shouted a familiar voice from outside the livery. "Willow McMurtry, are you in there? It's Daisy. We're here, sis!"

"Be right out," she yelled in reply. "Give me just a second. Got to gather my bags and straighten up a few things in here first."

"Remember it's raining," came a less easygoing voice.

"I'll hurry," she promised, hearing the impatience in Snow's voice. Willow wondered if Bear and his wife had had any hint of the fire. Had they been able to smell it? She asked Mr. Newcomb why he thought the blacksmith hadn't already come out to check on the odor.

"Don't worry about it. I'll explain what happened. He'll get a whiff once the rain stops. You need to go on with your sisters and get home while you can."

Grateful she could be in better sorts when she apologized to the blacksmith, Willow thanked Newcomb and pointed to the soiled blanket lying next to his duster. "I'll be glad to take those with me and wash them with this one. When I return the blankets, I'll bring back your coat, too."

"No need. I'll take care of them." He picked up

the items and grabbed the one she held as he headed to the door.

He didn't seem eager to have reason to visit her. She didn't know whether to be appreciative for his kindness about taking the washing off her hands or insulted that he wanted to avoid further contact with her as much as possible.

"We'll have to connect later on, then," she said, "after the wedding tomorrow. Unless you're a friend of my sisters or Bass Parker, my future brother-in-law. If you're invited to the wedding, we could visit a little at the reception. Maybe by then you'll have a decision about working for me?"

"I'm invited, but I'd rather talk you out of it. You're better off finding someone else to help you."

Her hands clapped softly together, ignoring his attempt to dissuade her. "The reception will give us some time at least to talk further."

And make it easier for Snow not to fuss with her about spending time with the stranger once Daisy and Bass left for their honeymoon. If he was already a friend of the family, then Snow would consider him a proper enough acquaintance to allow him into Daisy's home or to allow Willow to meet him in town.

How she disliked those times when she became little sister again, treated as though she must have a protective mother hen to watch over her. Willow couldn't wait until the day both Snow and Daisy saw her as grown and not the baby of the family. After all, she was relatively a spinster's age.

"Before you go, Willow—" Newcomb's use of her name revealed he'd listened well "—I've got one more question before I'll consider teaching you anything."

He's truly considering it!

Another fine trait to add to her characterization of Ketchum. *Note #2: Texas men pay close attention.* "And what question is that, Mr. Newcomb?"

"We're getting soaked out here," barked Snow, "and it's a long fifteen minutes home."

She and Snow loved each other but were as different as night and day. Being someone who preferred things calm, quiet and orderly, Snow had the hardest time putting up with Willow's slower efforts.

"I'll answer you in just a minute. We forgot to turn out the lantern. I'll be right there." Just as she reached to grab it, Willow saw where the daddy longlegs had taken up a new home and nearly knocked the lamp over.

"Owww, that's hot." She jerked her hand back but managed to keep from spilling the kerosene and setting another fire.

"You need help?" Newcomb demanded and turned around, her baggage in his hands.

"No! Everything's just fine. I'm right behind you." She used the edge of her petticoats for a pot holder and set the lantern on its base, turning off the key to the kerosene. For good measure, she blew at the wick just to make sure no flame remained.

"I'm sorry, horses," she whispered as she used the lightning flashes to help her see the way out to her sister's wagon. "I'll make it up to you tomorrow after the wedding if you're still here, okay? Don't know about you, but I need to calm way, way down. I know you will when I'm out of here."

When she reached her sisters, she found them sitting side by side on the driver's box. Snow shared a parasol with Daisy, but it did little to fight off the rain. Both started asking all kinds of questions.

"Let me thank Mr. Newcomb for his help," she told them. "Then I'll answer everything along the way, okay?"

"Of course," Daisy replied, appearing unwilling to turn around and greet them face to face. "Thank you, Gage, for lending her a hand. That's kind of you. Do forgive us for being so… Well, we took a chance on leaving our curlers in, hoping we'd be here so briefly that no one would actually see us except Willow, maybe Bear. He would understand, of course."

Gage. So that was his name. Willow filed it back in her memory for future reference.

"You all right?" he asked, targeting his question to Willow instead of making any comment about her sisters' embarrassment about their hair. He lifted her bags into the wagon, then offered Willow a hand up as she climbed in the back.

When their fingers touched, she winced. "I will be. The lantern was hot when I turned it off."

"Too sore to lasso a stump?" His eyes studied her carefully.

"No. I'm ready to learn from you. The quicker,

the better." If she hadn't known any differently, she'd have suspected he was trying to help her ease how angry she was with herself. But he didn't know her at all. *Note #3: Texas men sense when to lend a hand.*

"Then, as I started to ask before, I need your word that nobody's going to get hurt from me teaching you to shoot and everything else you've mentioned. That this involves nothing illegal."

Maybe he truly was a lawman of some kind.

"All I can say is that's my intention at the moment, but I'll be honest with you, partner." She gave her best nasal imitation of Texas twang. "My intentions get out of sorts more often than not. Will you just trust me on this?"

He mulled it over hard. Too hard, in her opinion. Maybe she'd have to ask someone else, but he seemed the perfect teacher.

"*Trust* is the key word here, Willow." He took off his hat and put it on top of her head. "Don't ever give me reason to doubt you."

She shuddered, either from the cool rain or the threat tempering the warning he'd just given her.

She tried to return the hat but he backed away.

"Next time it rains, bring a parasol with you. You'll stay a lot drier," he ordered, then headed toward Bear's quarters without giving her a definite yes.

Chapter Three

The wagon seemed to speed up despite the rain. Willow reached up and pulled Gage's hat down, making sure it didn't blow off.

"The horses are smelling home," Daisy announced. "They want out of this as much as we do."

Willow's heartbeat accelerated to match the team's eager gait. She was anxious to be done with the long day's travel. She hoped her sisters didn't question her about why she'd been in the livery with Gage. After all, he'd simply taken refuge from the storm, just as she had.

She wasn't sure how much, if anything, she was ready to tell them about the other reason she'd come to High Plains. Saying anything about hiring Gage Newcomb and her reason for doing so could wait until she was certain he agreed. Besides, she hadn't decided for sure she wouldn't change her mind and use someone else.

The team made a turn. A gust of wind whipped Gage's hat off Willow's head but she managed to grab it in time. Fearful that she'd lose it again, she tried to tuck it under one thigh, despite the rain. The wagon rocked and swayed hard, sending her sideways. Her hip crushed the hat crown.

She sat upright again, wondering if Gage would be more understanding about her accidentally crushing his hat than she'd been of the lady who'd done the same to hers.

Was there a way to fix it before he found out?

The man made her nervous. That was for sure. But a man like her character should make people want to right their wrongs, shouldn't he?

She crammed the hat back down on her head, hoping the crown would pop into shape again. Hardly. She'd have to try something else.

Disgust rode with her the rest of the way.

Finally, the horses stopped in front of a large two-story house with a couple of outbuildings and a corral. Willow exhaled a breath of appreciation as the journey ended.

"Shepard, we're here!" Daisy hailed, setting the brake. "Ollie, Thad, come grab a bag, will you? Tell Myrtle to warm up the coffee for us."

The rain chose that moment to stop.

"Naturally," Snow uttered in her sarcastic way and closed her parasol, revealing her normally solid-white hair had not been protected from the dampness of the rain.

From the barn, a man in a slouch hat, a shirt and chaps came running out to take the reins from Daisy. Willow noticed his black hair had a streak of gray running across the left temple.

"You done for the day, Mrs. Trumbo?" he asked, one of his gloved hands stroking the horse closest to him as if it were a treasured pet. "You want me to brush 'em down or will you be headed back to town for any reason?"

"I'm finished. We've still got too much to do before morning and I'm sure my groom doesn't need to see me looking like this." She headed to the back of the wagon to help Willow down. "Shepard, this is my sister Willow. Miss Willow McMurtry, my ranch hand, Mr. Shepard Hutton."

"Howdy."

The ranch hand tipped his hat and revealed eyes the color of cottonwood leaves when they shimmered in the wind. Silver-green. Freckles dotting his nose made him look younger than the gray streak implied. He was about a head shorter than she was, she'd guess, and she noted he stored a coiled bullwhip handle-up in one side of his holster, a gun in the other. He smiled and revealed a tooth on the left side that reminded her of a golden fang. The man exuded a curious mixture of innocence and danger about him. "Glad to meet you, miss."

What a man he'd make for either a hero or an outlaw! She couldn't wait to find out more about him and how he used his whip. Did handling animals require the use of one or was it simply a choice?

"I'm happy to meet you, Mr. Hutton." She held out her hand to shake his, but when she asked, "Have you worked for my sister long?" he didn't offer his in return.

She let her hand slide down to her side.

"Not long," he mumbled and started unloading cargo her sisters must have bought in town from the wagon.

Evasive, Willow delegated him in her notes. *Outlaw. Has manners Ketchum would never display.*

Willow was just about to ask Daisy and Snow how long they'd known the man but stopped when two little children came charging out the front door of house.

"Aunt Willow," exclaimed the little blonde girl in braids and overalls, throwing her arms around her in greeting. Genuine welcome shone in her amber-colored eyes. "'Zit true ya came all the way from Florida to watch us?"

"Actually, I've been in Geor—" Willow almost said too much, but she refused to lie to her niece. Instead, she said, "I'd come a lot farther to take care of you if you needed me."

And she meant it. She should have already been in Ollie's and Thad's lives long before now. She'd make sure she made her stay here with them memorable and something they would never forget…but in a good way.

Willow hadn't expected Ollie to be so friendly

right off. A refreshing prospect after Gage's bent of bossiness.

Her niece barely knew her. Daisy must have been kind in relating anything about her to the children. For that she'd always be grateful to her sister. She wanted them to enjoy being with her, and now she wanted both to miss her if she ever left.

But Thaddeus didn't seem enthusiastic at all about her arrival. He didn't hug her, just grabbed one of her bags, as his mother had instructed.

"Thank you for taking that in for me." She tried to make him comfortable with talking to her. He was the spitting image of his late father—sandy-colored hair and gray eyes. But she'd never known Knox Trumbo to be shy, especially around women.

Daisy had said the boy had been orphaned by both his parents, but her sister still hadn't revealed how she'd learned about the existence of her now-adopted son.

The fact that Thad and Ollie were the same age stirred lots of speculation in Willow's overactive imagination, but she would wait to satisfy her curiosity until Daisy was ready to talk about those circumstances.

"Oh, yeah, I'm s'posed to grab the other bag." Ollie unwrapped her arms from around Willow's waist. "Mama said I get to show you which room you're sleeping in. You'll like it real good. I made sure I cleaned out the spiders and stuff."

"Spiders? What kind of stuff?" Willow had heard

about some of her niece's antics from Daisy's letters through the years. Where Willow's mishaps were accidental, Ollie seemed to have a knack for deliberate shenanigans that went awry.

Hopefully, there would be no more meetings with Texas spiders for the rest of this trip.

"Ollie-Golly likes to play jokes on people." Thaddeus glared at his sister. "Especially me. I told her you might be one of them prissy ladies who don't like bugs and worms and crawfish or fleas in your taters."

"Thaddy-Wumpus ain't no do-gooder either. He's trained Butler, our goat, to catch you bent over and—"

"Olivia Jane Trumbo, you two have got two months to catch your aunt up on all those wonderful little details." Snow McMurtry interrupted the list of torture techniques each child had devised for the other. "Now, why don't the both of you do what your mama asked? Let's settle Willow in and we all can meet in the parlor once we've changed out of these wet clothes. Shepard, go ahead and put up the team and wagon."

The ranch hand took the reins and started to lead the team away.

"I ain't changin' no clothes. I ain't wet." Ollie eyed Willow's raggedy appearance. "You don't look like you'd mind much."

Willow suddenly realized the ranch hand had seen her like this and she'd totally forgotten how she appeared. No wonder he hadn't wanted to shake her hand. Maybe she'd been too quick to criticize his standoffishness.

"I don't much mind at all, but your aunt Snow's right. I'd appreciate some sprucing-up time. Is that okay with you? I don't normally look this bad."

"You don't look bad, Miss McMurtry," Shepard called back over his shoulder. "I think you'll clean up real good."

"Why, thank you, Mr. Hutton. I'll certainly try my best." When he disappeared into the barn with the team, she smiled, deciding maybe he could be a good sort after all. Maybe he could teach her a thing or two about the way Texas men treated ladies, especially if Gage Newcomb chose not to. Or she didn't take Gage on after all.

Daisy and Snow shared a glance and laughed. Willow knew that look too well. Matchmaking thrived in their blood anytime the three sisters were together but particularly now, when a wedding was already on their minds.

They didn't understand she had no interest in marrying yet. Not until she had value of her own and didn't need to count on being Mrs. Somebody to be respected.

Willow had a certain kind of man in mind if she ever married. One who valued her opinion and never judged her. Most important, she wanted him to need her. She could never love a man who could live a better life without her. Until she came across such a man, she'd just be a spinster aunt.

"Uh-uh," she told them, heading inside, "you can

just put those thoughts out of your head. I'm here to watch over the children, not find a man."

A believable character, maybe, but not a husband.

"May I speak to your husband, ma'am?" Gage eyed the blacksmith's wife and waited for her to allow him to step inside their quarters. The fragrance of ginger cookies permeated the air, reminding him that he hadn't eaten anything today and needed to. That would have to wait even longer. Though he looked wetter than a duck in a flood and needed to get out of his soaked clothes, he'd made a promise to Willow McMurtry and he'd keep it.

"It won't take but a minute," he promised, wishing he still had his hat so he could pull it down and spare Pigeon the sight of his scars.

But then Willow would have had to ride back home without anything to protect her from the rain. That that caused him any concern had been as much a surprise to him as offering to clean the blankets for her. She brought out a consideration for people he thought he'd lost in long years of riding herd on criminals.

Bear's wife pulled her shawl a little closer around her but stepped aside and let him in. "The rain cooled things off some."

"Sure did, ma'am."

She wore a frailty about her. Her rosy cheeks looked flushed from fever, not good health, and her breathing seemed shallow and brief.

"Mind if I stay right here on your rug so I don't

track up your floors? Wouldn't want to put you to any more trouble."

"No trouble." She smiled kindly, but her eyes looked tired, her gray hair braided to one side as if secured for bedtime even though it was barely late afternoon.

"Come on in and pull up Bear's rocker next to the fire. Dry yourself off some and I'll fetch my husband. He's sorting the mail, getting it ready to post over at the mercantile and such." She excused herself and went into a room farther back in the cozy decorated home.

Gage knew *and such* meant that on the days the stage didn't run, the smithy made a habit of taking mail to folks he knew who had a hard time picking it up from the mail slots located at the mercantile for that purpose.

At first, Gage had thought Bear was too eager to help out with the mail and wondered why. But then he'd discovered that Bear and Pigeon always handed out ginger cookies to the children who waited while their parents read letters and decided whether they would write one in reply. The couple lent a hand in reading or writing the missives for those who couldn't do so themselves. Gage thought the Funderburgs were some of the kindest people he'd ever met. He promised himself before he left High Plains for good, he would find out what had spurred their need for such kindness.

"Yes? How can I help you?" Bear entered the main

room, his gaze sweeping over Gage as he sat in the chair holding his gloveless hand out to warm it.

Gage started to stand but the blacksmith motioned him to remain seated and pulled his wife's rocker alongside.

The rocker creaked with the smithy's great size as he sat. "Glad to have some company. Pardon my missus. She's not up to visiting and asked that I give you her apologies. Trying to save her energy for the Parker wedding tomorrow. But she did manage some cookies, if you'd like one or two. I could scrounge up some coffee or tea, if you like."

A cookie and something to drink sounded wonderful, but Gage didn't think it fair to take the man's hospitality when he was about to tell him they'd nearly burned down his livery.

"No, thanks. I promised a friend I'd pass along a message to you. We ought to get on with that so you can get back to your sorting. Warming up is good, though."

"I saw you watching our newest arrival earlier." Bear rocked back and forth. "This got anything to do with Willow McMurtry?"

Surprise filled Gage. It shouldn't have. From all he'd noticed about Bear through his weeks in High Plains, the smithy seemed to know everyone's comings or goings. Of course he would pay attention to someone like him standing around eyeing people, not taking up work anywhere.

Bear probably wondered what he did for a living.

No one in the area knew for sure except Teague, his fellow Ranger, whom he had helped in catching some local bank robbers. The engaged couple might have a clue he was part of Texas's Special Forces, but if they did, they hadn't disclosed that fact to anyone yet.

"Yeah, I'm here about her." Gage told Bear how he'd taken shelter from the rain, about the accidental fire and how they'd managed to get it under control. "We didn't want you to go in and wonder what had happened. She didn't want to leave before making it right with you, but it was as much my fault as hers. So I told her I'd take care of telling you."

He looked the smithy in the eyes. "I think I startled her when I came in and made her drop the match. I'd like to offer to pay for the damage or see who you think could best repair the wall. I'll hire them to do the job. I'd do it myself but I'm not that good at carpentry."

Gage didn't know if he would be able to see well enough to repair the wall.

Bear put his palms on his knees and rocked back and forth, studying the fire. "I think I'll take you up on that offer, friend. The Trumbo brothers are excellent carpenters. Together, they could have a wall replaced in an hour, maybe two. You sure it's safe and will hold until tomorrow or the next day?"

Gage nodded. "I checked it close enough. It'll hold."

"Good. Then I have a request for you."

"Name it." The smithy was being fair about the

whole situation. Anything Bear asked would seem trivial to building a wall.

"I have some mail that needs to be delivered to Daisy and her sister. Wished I'd heard them before they took off for home. I guess I was so concentrated on the mail I didn't hear them come or go. But I do have it sorted enough to give them theirs. Daisy's been getting all kinds of correspondence since making wedding plans, and what with her intended inviting half the territory, who knows if these are important letters to read before the wedding or not? I'm a bit surprised Miss Willow's received one so soon."

"Somebody wanted to make sure the letter was here on her arrival. Wonder why," Gage speculated aloud.

"Hard to guess," Bear answered, "but if you agree to deliver the letters for me, maybe you can discover the answer to that. I wouldn't have to leave Pigeon by herself and you could find out from Daisy if her brothers-in-law plan to be at the wedding. If she says they will, you could ask them yourself if they want the work. Sometimes they do. Sometimes you couldn't pay them enough to keep them inside anywhere."

Gage understood that. He'd spent his life reading trails. He understood the wide-open and limitless distance and felt cooped up anytime he was inside. Losing his sight would definitely narrow his ranging space.

No time to feel sorry for himself. He could get his hat sooner if he delivered the letters, maybe get back in time to get it cleaned up and dried enough to attend the ceremony.

Quit kidding yourself, Newcomb, he told himself. *You're hankering to see Willow sooner than you thought.* There was no reason whatsoever not to wait until morning to make the delivery. He could speak to the Trumbo brothers at the reception. If they didn't attend, somebody would know where to find them. From what he'd heard and seen of them, the brothers weren't exactly men who kept themselves inconspicuous.

Surely no letter was so important that it was worth disrupting the preparations for the wedding or putting himself in danger of revealing his weakness. What if the rain continued for most of the evening and he lost his way in the downpour? How would he explain that to anyone and offer a logical reason without arousing speculation?

One nagging thought kept bothering Gage. What if that insistent letter to Willow had anything at all to do with Stanton Hodge? A wedding might be perfect to bring the snake out of his den to strike while everyone in town was distracted.

He couldn't take the chance on waiting to find out.

Then again, he could be wrong, and she could have no connection at all to the man.

Gage finally rose from the rocker. There was only one thing a Ranger could do.

Sink spur and ride saddle till he found the right road to take.

"Hand me those letters. I better get them on out

there while I can. Looks like it means to give us a good dunking or three before the clouds move on past."

Bear disappeared into the next room and returned with both envelopes. "Here you go. Hope it's worth the trouble you're putting yourself through."

"By the way, I need to mention one more thing." A chill swept over Gage as he moved away from the warmth of Bear's hearth. "If you see a man fitting this description, would you keep me posted? Not quite six foot, red hair long enough to tie back. Green eyes, if you can ever get him to look you in the face. Both hands are scarred but he's fair with a pistol. Deadly with a whip."

"A wanted man?" Bear opened his door to let Gage leave.

Gage stepped outside and faced the blacksmith. "More than most. One way you'll spot him easy— when he grins, he's got a shiny tooth. Considers himself a ladies' man and likes to show it off as some kind of prized nugget he won from a miner."

"What'd he do?"

"Rustled horses."

"You plan to kill him?"

Though Gage could legally take justice into his own hands, he shook his head. "He'll face a judge."

"Were they your horses?"

"No." Gage stared Bear straight in the eyes, not caring that his scars were in full sight. "He stole my future. Worst kind of thief there is."

Chapter Four

Willow was surprised to discover she had been assigned a room by herself. From the number of people now living in Daisy's house—Daisy, Snow, Ollie, Thaddeus and a family housekeeper named Myrtle—Willow had assumed she would be sharing accommodations with somebody.

Sharing a room with her sisters all her life and listening to them breathe at night had always given her the comfort of knowing that she wasn't alone. Working in Atlanta and renting a room at the boardinghouse had been a real challenge because she had to brave the night noises alone. Something she knew she must conquer at some point if she was to ever make a success of living on her own.

For tonight, Daisy and Snow would be only a room or two away, so it wasn't as if she'd really be alone in a houseful of strangers.

Snow liked everything kept in perfect order and

free of clutter. Willow did, too, but it wasn't something she quite managed. She took a look around the room. Her soggy dress lay in an emerald pile on the braided rug next to the quilt-covered four-poster bed. As soon as the children had toted in her baggage and left her alone, she'd quickly changed. An inspection of her belongings in the damp baggage had offered one blue frock that seemed dry enough to make her presentable for the rest of the evening. She would have to heat up Daisy's irons and press the remainder of her clothes before she had anything to wear to the wedding.

A small washstand connected to an armoire housed a flowered pitcher and matching bowl that provided water and a place to wash the remaining soot off her face and hands. The towel she'd found in one of the drawers now stretched across the quilt, streaked with evidence that she'd arrived looking like a raccoon that had rummaged in a chimney full of cinders.

After thorough brushes through her thick hair, she'd had to leave the curls down to let them dry and hope they would before morning so she could wear them up for the wedding.

Yes, maybe it was good that she didn't have to share rooms with Snow tonight. Her sister would gripe on first sight of this mess. But if Snow stayed true to form, Willow should be able to crack her door open just enough to hear her sister snoring all the way down the hall. That ought to be reassuring enough to maintain a sense of ease for the night.

"Are you about finished up there, Willow?" Daisy

called from the parlor below. "The meal's ready and you need to eat while it's hot. Thaddeus, come to the table, please. Make sure your hands are washed."

"What about Ollie?" His voice echoed from nearby.

"Worry about yourself, son."

"Be right down." Willow glanced at the messy room and promised herself she would tidy up later just in case the children wanted to come in and wish her good-night. She wanted to start things off right with them.

Thinking of asking Daisy about the heating irons, she grabbed Gage's hat and decided to try her best to press it back into shape.

She exited her room, taking a good look down the hall to find which direction would lead her to the staircase.

"This way." Thaddeus poked his head around a corner and pointed behind him. "I got lost a couple of nights when I first got here. If you want me to—" he dug into his pocket and pulled out a small knife "—I'll mark an X on the wall so you'll remember it's thisaway."

"That won't be necessary," she told him, hurrying to catch up while counting how many bedrooms she passed so she would remember which one she'd been assigned. Encouraging him to carve a direction would not sit well with his mother. Maybe she'd better ask Daisy if she knew about the knife. "You can put that away."

He shrugged. "Okay, but don't blame me if you get lost or fall."

Images of her stumbling made Willow grab the railing securely once they reached the stairs. No need to take chances.

"Who's going to fall?" asked Ollie as she swept past Willow, turned backward and straddled the banister. "You can always sli-ide down and have fun!" She gave a rowdy "Yee-haw!" as she slid to the first floor.

Watching her precocious niece the next two months would take some real concentration, Willow realized. The eight-year-old seemed fearless.

"You two quit trying to ruffle your aunt's feathers and get to the table right now," ordered a pleasantly plump salt-and-pepper-haired woman who met them at the bottom of the stairs. Dressed in a paisley skirt, butternut blouse and an apron, she carried a picnic basket covered with a checkered cloth.

The delicious aromas wafting from beneath the cloth made Willow's stomach constrict with hunger and reminded her that she had not eaten since sunrise. Her stomach had churned back and forth with the sway of the coach all day and nearly made her lose breakfast once or twice. She had thought it would take a week for her appetite to return.

"Howdy-do, Miss Willow. I'm Myrtle, your sister's cook and housekeeper," the woman said. "I'd curtsy but I got my hands full. I know Daisy's told you some about me in her letters but we'll get to know each other well, I expect. Go on in and have you some supper. I'll be right back."

She lifted one cowboy boot she wore and scratched the back of her other leg with its tooled instep. Some of Daisy's leatherwork? Willow wondered.

"Excuse me, I got an itch I can't reach proper," the cook apologized. "Now, as I was saying, Shepard takes meals on his own, not with the family, and I like him to eat while it's hot. I think he prefers being with those horses better than he does us gals, if you ask me. Can't convince him to come in and join us. And you won't find me a badgering kind of gal."

"Aww, you're sweet on him, Myrtie," Ollie teased, "and you know it."

The cook spun on her booted heels and headed out the door, calling back over her shoulder, "Don't try hitching this old goose to a young gander like that, Little Miss Matchmaker. You'll run him off, and we need him to stay till your mom and new daddy come back home."

"I ain't making no promises," Ollie warned.

"And I ain't helping you do nothing. It always gets me in big trouble," Thaddeus threatened.

"How about we leave poor Mr. Hutton and your cook alone to make their own choices," Willow suggested, deciding it best to let the children know she wouldn't allow them to interfere with anything the two employees had in mind while Daisy was gone.

As a hopeful writer, she thought it would be interesting to explore all sorts of relationships. Why couldn't an older woman fall in love with a slightly younger man? Didn't older men tend to take younger wives? "I'm sure they both know exactly what they're doing without any help from us."

Just as she and the children headed for the kitchen table, a knock sounded at the door. Willow halted and glanced back, wondering if the cook had forgotten something and returned to get it. She hadn't had time to deliver the basket to the barn yet, had she? But why would she be knocking?

"I'll get it," Ollie informed them.

"You two get in here and let Willow answer it," demanded Snow. "You're just trying to avoid eating. I've already checked the potatoes. Nobody's done anything to them. You're safe."

What in the world did that mean? Willow wondered as both children moaned and obeyed their aunt's command. Willow crossed the room, opened the door and instantly recognized their visitor, her hand shoving his hat behind her back.

Gage Newcomb.

"What are you doing here?" Her thought spewed from her mouth as if someone had primed a pump in her brain.

His hand lifted toward his forehead as if reaching for his hat, then quickly returned to his side. He simply nodded a brief hello and asked, "May I come in?"

She had his hat. He couldn't thumb it up as any Texan might do in greeting. She'd wanted to have it repaired before she saw him again. "Just a moment."

Willow turned and called to her sister, "Daisy, are you receiving company tonight?"

Daisy came around the corner, taking off her apron. When she saw their visitor's identity, she unconsciously reached up to touch the curlers in her hair. "Please do come in."

Thankful he opened the door the rest of the way himself, Willow kept both hands on the hat and turned her body as he stepped inside.

"Have you been to supper?" Daisy waved an arm toward the kitchen. "We were just about to sit down and eat. Myrtle made plenty. Won't you join us?"

He glanced at Willow as if seeking whether she had any objections. Not that she would voice them, being that she was just as much a guest in her sister's house as he was. Maybe this would give her an opportunity to ask him a few more needed questions.

His tongue darted out to lick his bottom lip. "I'm obliged, Widow Trumbo. I guess it's time I stop referring to you as that from now on, isn't it?"

Daisy laughed. "Tomorrow's soon enough. Now, please, come grab a chair and tell us all why we have the pleasure of your company."

He gave a brief explanation, ending with, "Mrs. Funderburg wasn't feeling well and Bear didn't want to leave her alone, so I agreed to bring the letters to you."

"I'm sorry to hear that about Pigeon." Sincerity filled Daisy's tone.

Chivalrous, Willow added to the mental notes for her character. *Thoughtful of others*. A new view of

Gage was emerging. He was a mixture of behaviors and that made him real. Already she could see ways to improve Ketchum's character and make readers like him better.

When Gage followed Daisy to the kitchen, Willow quickly deposited his hat on the pegged rack stationed near the front door. Maybe he wouldn't notice it later among the variety of colored bonnets hanging there, but the hat looked boldly masculine in contrast to the feminine headwear. The crumpled crown couldn't go unnoticed long. When she finally joined everyone at the table, she was surprised to find Gage remained standing with a chair pulled out for her.

"Thank you," she muttered, pleased that he was on his best behavior and displaying good manners.

Gage sat down next to her, his long legs accidentally touching hers beneath the table due to the crowded circle of diners. Willow supposed sitting saddled for long periods of riding would bow a tall man's legs. She'd have to remember that. Willow glanced up and her eyes met his for a brief second before she inched away to give him more room. He certainly looked uncomfortable, and she wasn't sure if it was purely from being crowded.

Daisy scooped roast beef and potatoes with onions and brown gravy onto each plate, offering Gage a man-sized portion. "There's sweet carrots and celery, too. I'll let you take what you like and pass the bowl down. Oh, and the sourdough biscuits and butter are sitting next to Snow's plate. We have mint tea or milk, if you like, or I can make coffee."

"Whatever's already made, ma'am. I appreciate any of it."

Daisy handed Willow two glasses. "The pitcher's closer to you. Will you pour the milk, please?"

No, Willow wished she could say, not trusting her hand to be steady enough to do a good job. Instead, she snaked her fingers out and latched on to the pitcher's handle and tilted it to one side, hoping to connect the rim to the top of Gage's glass without having to actually lift the pitcher.

She hadn't expected it to be so full and her fingers slipped, sending a splash of milk crashing over the glass to land atop the mound of roast beef on his plate.

She groaned, her eyes closing in utter embarrassment, only to spring open again so she could see what she was doing.

"Here, let me help you," he offered, his fingers wrapping around hers to take the weight from the pitcher and allow her to pour more accurately. As he leaned into her, their shoulders touched and she became aware of how chiseled his bearded jaw appeared at this angle. The slope of his nose looked patrician and the scars around his eyes were too welted for Willow not to feel a twinge of pity for him.

His shoulders straightened as if he'd taken notice of her thoughts, and he purposefully inched away. She knew she'd overstepped his boundary by staring and was sorry she hadn't caught herself before he became aware of her gaze tracing his features.

He grabbed his glass in the other hand and tilted it so the milk could flow inside without either of them having to be that close together again.

Willow didn't know what to do to set him at ease, but when she started to offer an apology, Gage waved away her words. He simply stirred the milk that soaked his plate, mixing it into a thinner gravy that was a lighter shade of brown.

"A little milk won't hurt," he announced.

But she'd seen the truth and not heeded the warning he'd given in the livery earlier.

Pity was something he would not tolerate.

Rain kept a steady beat on the roof and streaked across the window that had been raised to let out heat from the stove. Just as Gage had assumed, the ride back to town would now have its challenges if the storm kept up after nightfall. It was getting hard enough to see in the dark. It would be even harder with the trail further blurred by rainfall. On the other hand, he felt out of place inside among walls. He'd lived so much of his life out in the open and on the trail that he couldn't wait to be on his way out of here. He had to force himself to take time eating.

He wanted nothing more than to deliver the letters, collect his hat and get back to town before sundown, but he couldn't ask Willow and Daisy to read the letters until they were ready to accept them.

No one appeared even remotely interested in the mail. Maybe the trip out here could have waited until morning.

However, Willow seemed intent on making him linger, offering second helpings, asking him questions and appearing genuinely interested in getting to know him better.

Was she afraid she'd offended him earlier and that he would decide not to teach her any of the skills she wanted to learn? Maybe that was why she was making the most of questioning him now.

Though he'd let his temper rule him when he caught her looking sympathetically at his face, he regretted acting so small. It wasn't her fault he was touchy on the subject. He just preferred that no one get a good enough look to speculate on whether or not he would recover from the damage. That was nobody's business but his.

Trouble was, in twenty-eight years of living, he'd never learned how to say he was sorry about anything. Thought it made him look weak. Maybe he could just stick around awhile to show he had no hard feelings and he had better manners.

Living life as a Ranger hadn't required him to question his reactions before. Gage didn't like the fact that he was doing it now.

He laid down his fork and pushed back his chair so he could gather his plate and glass. "Need help with the dishes?" He couldn't remember the last time he'd ever made such an offer.

Daisy gathered the children's empty plates along with her own. "That's kind of you, but we'll get to these later."

"I'll take care of them," the cook said. "Y'all move into the parlor and see what's in those letters. I'm sure he's in a hurry to be on his way."

Gage was glad he didn't have to make good on his offer.

The widow's small daughter piped up. "Why don't ya just stay the night, Mr. Gage? You can bunk in the barn with Shepard or out under the stars with Bass. We'll unsaddle your horse tied out front and put him in an empty stall."

Daisy looked askance at Gage as she put the dishes in a wash tin and wiped her hands on a cloth. "You're certainly most welcome to. We have a couple of extra bunks out there and fresh blankets."

Everyone but the cook headed for the parlor.

"I appreciate the offer." Gage took a seat in one of the high-backed chairs across from a flowered settee. "But I'm sure you ladies still have plenty to do before the wedding tomorrow. I don't want to get in your way. I'll just hand you these envelopes and wait and see if you need me to take back a reply. Oh, and—" he glanced at Willow, who was moving closer to the front door as he spoke "—I'd appreciate picking up my hat if you're finished with it."

Light from the parlor lamp shone on the livery burner's hair, making him see it well for the first time. Streaks the color of the July sun baking the earth filtered through the wealth of curls she'd combed and set free from her earlier upswept tangle. Not quite blond yet nowhere near red, the peculiar color matched her somehow. Odd yet pretty. She needed to leave it down.

"Y-you'll have to give me a moment," she stammered. "I'll need to see what I did with it and—"

"Right there, Aunt Willow." Thaddeus pointed to the rack she had positioned herself in front of. "Looks like ya broke it."

Willow grabbed the hat. "Just give me a moment, Mr. Newcomb, and it will be perfectly fine. The stove's hot and my sister has the irons heating already." She turned to Daisy. "May I use one of them?"

"Of course. Just make sure you reheat whatever you use when you're done." Daisy exhaled a long breath. "I still have a lot of pressing to do before I go to bed tonight."

"Ahh, Mama, you don't have to iron nothing for me. I'm gonna get it wrinkled up anyway," complained Ollie. "You know I will."

Snow fumbled with one of her rollers. "My hair will never dry like this by morning. I might as well take these out and use the irons instead. Or better yet, make you help me curl it before the wedding," she grumbled as Willow moved past. "You're the reason it's still wet, remember?"

When Willow spun around and faced her complaining sister, Gage noted each definitely had some sort of issue with the other. But as long as there was no gunfire involved, it wasn't his concern.

"Just let me take care of Mr. Newcomb's hat and I'll be more than happy to help with your hair," Willow said sweetly before disappearing into the kitchen.

An admirable effort, Gage thought, probably to not appear quarrelsome in front of the children.

But from the sound of the banging and clanging of irons against the stovetop, she didn't have any better handle on her temper than he had earlier. A dangerous situation considering Willow had already proven herself too clumsy for her own good.

"Watch out!" yelled the cook. "You're going to—"

"Now I've gone and done it. Mr. Newcomb, can you come in here a minute?" Willow wailed from the kitchen.

The children raced to see, but Daisy stood and held them back. "You two go upstairs and get your clothes laid out for tomorrow. I'll be up to check on you in a bit."

As the children complained but complied, Gage raised a palm, motioning Daisy to wait. He reached into his vest pocket and pulled out the letters. "Here— why don't you read this while I help her? The other one's for Willow. I've got a clue what's happened in there, so no need for you to concern yourself."

Daisy accepted the letters, and the rip of the envelope being opened behind him gave Gage hope that coming here might prove worth the time. His goal now was to see what emergency Willow had gotten herself into and get her out quick enough so she could read her letter, too.

He stuck his head around the kitchen doorway. One look confirmed what he'd suspected. His hat dangled from a forefinger on her right hand, a hole burned into the crumbled crown where she'd attempted to press it into shape. The irons had been too hot.

He moved toward her, lifted the hat from her finger and settled it on his head. Now he'd have to pay a visit to the mercantile and see if there were any replacements in stock or if he'd have to go without one until he could order it in from Fort Worth or Mobeetie.

Willow's gaze swept up to study him and he let her see that though the thought of having to bare his face to everybody would be an irritating prospect, he refused to overreact to the loss of a hat.

"Maybe the first skill I ought to teach you, Miss McMurtry, is how to handle something hot," he suggested. "From what I've seen so far, you could use a little more practice in that area."

Her chin tilted as challenge flared in her eyes. "Got wisdom on how to control a temper, do you?"

She had some bite in her beak, and he deserved the pecking for criticizing her. He made a mental note to go easier on that as he taught her, but he wasn't about to admit that he'd lost his temper with her earlier. "If I don't have enough already, I'm sure I will have by the time we get through with the lessons you want," he answered her.

"So you've made up your mind you'll teach me?"

"Long as you'll stay away from my next hat." He liked a good challenge and keeping her close would assure him she had no other motive than just to learn.

She paused a moment as if she was reconsidering her offer. Finally, she held out her hand and said, "Deal."

He shook her hand and noticed she was doing her best to grip as though she had the strength of a man. He admired her bravado, but he eased up on his own grip so he wouldn't crush her confidence. "Deal."

"You two sound like you better tread carefully in whatever you're planning," the cook warned, her voice cracking like thunder as she continued washing dishes, "or you'll find yourselves in more trouble than either of you can handle."

Gage knew a formidable opponent when he met one. He saw that Myrtle had already taken Willow under her wing and assigned herself as chief protector of Daisy's family while the bride honeymooned. If he discovered Willow guilty of any involvement with the horse thief and Myrtle didn't like the way he handled the situation, there was nothing more dangerous than an angry woman with an iron skillet defending her own.

"Duly warned, ma'am." He tipped the edge of his battered hat.

"I suspect we ought to be seeing about those letters now," Willow encouraged, setting the irons back into proper order to reheat.

Gage moved aside to let her pass, glad she was the one who mentioned putting an end to the evening so he could hurry back to town. As they returned to the parlor, he noticed Daisy had already finished reading her letter. She handed the other one to Willow.

"Who do you know in Georgia?" Curiosity colored Daisy's tone as she peered at Willow. Then her attention immediately swept to Gage's hat. "Oh, my, there's no fixing that, is there?"

Willow sat and busied herself in opening her letter, then scanned it instead of giving any explanation concerning the hat.

Gage decided there was no reason to dig the spur in deeper. "It'll hold off some of the rain until I get back to town. Just about worn it threadbare anyway. 'Bout time to buy a new one."

He watched Willow fold her letter and put it back in the envelope, clearly having not read all the pages. "Do either of you need me to take back a reply?"

Willow glanced up at him, looking startled and shoving the envelope deep into the pocket of her dress.

"I don't," Daisy announced, taking his attention away from her sister for just a moment. The future bride's lips broke into a radiant smile. "It's a confirmation of a surprise I have for Bass. Mother and Father are going to join us in Saint Louis since they couldn't be here for the wedding. I can't wait for Bass to meet them."

"I'll wait until next time I go to town to mail my answer," Willow replied quickly, then turned the conversation back to Daisy's excitement about joining their parents.

Gage's gaze returned to find Willow's hands locked together in her lap, one of her legs bouncing slightly. The evening had proven to be a waste of his time. Willow had never answered her sister about who she knew in Georgia and had seemed far too quick to put the missive away.

Every sense within him told Gage she was definitely hiding something and plenty nervous about it.

But what?

And about whom?

And why didn't she want anyone to know?

A sense of time ticking away filled Gage with an urgency to be about his business. Only God knew the hour his vision would go, when his skills would become more a danger than a service to anyone.

Whatever her deception, he could use Willow McMurtry to sharpen his waning abilities until Hodge made his next move.

It seemed everyone in this part of Texas had been invited to the wedding tomorrow, providing the perfect opportunity for the thief to show himself as friend or foe to Willow.

Something about Willow McMurtry was setting Gage's instincts on alert.

He sensed she was about to give him more problems than putting out a fire or buying a new hat.

Question now was, did whatever she hid about her letter have anything to do with *his* connection to Hodge?

Chapter Five

Charged with keeping Daisy's wedding bouquet safe from harm, Willow stood apart from everyone to make sure she protected it from others moving about.

She watched guests carrying platters of food and wedding gifts down the flower-strewn slope that led to the location behind Daisy's home where the wedding would take place. Daisy had told her that she and Bass had once shared a picnic here that had started them on the path to true love. They wanted to pay honor to her first husband, who had unknowingly brought them together. Knox Trumbo now rested in the family cemetery a roll of prairie beyond them.

While Daisy and her groom greeted their guests, others visited and chatted, layering the air with anticipation.

Willow spotted Gage Newcomb talking to the three Viking-sized men surrounding the blacksmith and a woman who must be the smithy's wife, for he wrapped his arm around her protectively.

The McMurtrys had grown up in Florida with the Trumbo brothers, so she remembered these three well. Daisy had married Knox, the oldest of the four brothers, and at his urging she'd set up home in Texas. Though the surviving brothers looked tough as rawhide with their tanned skin, sun-streaked hair and broken noses, they had a soft spot in their hearts for her oldest sister and her children. That made them good people to Willow, no matter how rough they appeared.

Gage wore a different hat today and looked handsome in the Sunday-go-to-meeting clothes he'd apparently bought for the occasion. Of course, he wouldn't have worn the smoke-stained duster or the hot-ironed holey hat she'd ruined. Later, when they talked, Willow would ask what he'd paid for the replacements and see that she reimbursed him for the expense.

She raised the bridal bouquet to her nose to ward off the memory of the fire and embarrassment that she still felt for having caused the damage.

Her attention shifted from Gage to the sweet verbena, the purplish-pink flowers with white centers that obviously meant something special to Daisy and Bass. The verbena graced the bouquet and every table as centerpieces, and they interlaced the arbor built for the couple to stand beneath while taking their vows.

The choice of location and flowers couldn't have been more beautiful, in her opinion, as long as the morning insects stayed their distance. She'd been surprised to learn the little white church in town would not be used for the setting, but now that she saw the size of the crowd, she could easily understand the decision to hold the wedding here.

The stream that meandered from near the homestead through the property to pool into a small lake provided a sun-kissed reflection of the bright Texas morning. Even the crosses and stone marker that stood in the cemetery just beyond the chosen site gave the place a sense of sacredness that honored the proceeding.

Blue-speckled pots hung from iron triangles over a line of small campfires meant to keep coffee hot and plentiful, while milk chilled in bottles down at the water's edge for those wanting something cold to drink.

Tables laden with breakfast foods of all kinds tempted Willow to take a bite or two, but Myrtle and some of the townswomen who'd offered to help serve already had their hands full swatting away the fingers of eager children. Not wanting to present a bad example for Ollie and Thad, Willow elected to mind her manners and concentrate on the one task she'd been assigned.

This was the first wedding she'd attended where the reception would take place before the wedding rather than after. She stored the images and senses away for writing down later. Her boss and readers would savor the details that added to the Texas experience.

There were important things to concentrate on

this morning, like making sure she got through her part of the ceremony, handing over the bouquet to Daisy. Without mishap.

Determined to think positive, Willow sucked in a deep breath of morning air.

Just as she refocused on the people rather than the enticing food, her breath caught and she thought she would choke. There, walking toward her, was Ellie Finchmeister, Atlanta's most notorious gossip.

Why on earth was she here?

Don't do anything wrong in front of her.

She has no clue you wrote the stories about Ketchum.

Maybe she doesn't really see you and she's headed toward someone else.

Willow started backing up as her mind raced on how to dodge Ellie. She bumped a table and heard a slosh.

Willow turned to discover a huge bowl of pink punch and the largest cake she'd ever seen. Punch now stained the tablecloth but had missed the bouquet. Not so fortunate with the cake. Buttery icing dotted the verbena, leaving one side of the cake stripped barren.

A gnat landed on the bouquet and Willow shook it off. Would Daisy have to swat bugs away until the moment she tossed the bouquet to hopeful contenders?

The morning had started out so well. Willow had been determined to prove she could get through this one day without causing any harm and prove herself capable. Would that day ever come?

"Yoo-hoo, Miss McMurtry!" The reed-thin Georgia native raised the fan she held and waved it at Willow. "Is that really you?"

No, it's someone else, Willow wanted to say to the gossip, whose nose seemed to extend the length of her reputation. But it would be rude to ignore her. That would just set Ellie into undue speculation. Best to get this over with.

While Willow waited for her to catch up, she attempted to wipe icing from the petals and only ended up breaking off a cluster. After Willow tried to hide the gap, the bouquet began looking poorly and Willow wasn't sure where to wipe the stickiness from her hands. She needed to find a cloth, fast. But Ellie finally reached her and Willow didn't want to have to explain why she must leave so quickly.

Offering the best smile she could muster, she announced, "I'm surprised to see you here, Ellie."

Ellie's brown eyes lit with excitement. "Oh, this wedding has been all the talk since I arrived to visit my aunt. You probably know her as Esther Sue Jenkins."

Willow shook her head. "I haven't met her yet."

"You will. She's quite well respected here in High Plains, I'm told."

Willow could imagine an older version of Ellie and shuddered. People infatuated with their own importance were the worst of gossips. Had Ellie inherited her tendencies from her relative, as Willow had from her own grandfather?

"So your aunt knows my sister and that's why you're here?" Willow asked.

Ellie pointed her fan in the direction of an elderly woman walking down the slope dressed in funeral black. "Yes, in fact, she's certain she played a part in bringing the bride and groom together. I can't wait to get back to Atlanta and tell everyone I actually got to attend Bass Parker's wedding. You know he's one of the wealthiest men in the social register. A captain of industry, I'm told." She flicked her fan open again and gave a little wink. "But then, your sister must have already made you aware of that, I'm sure."

"Actually, no. I didn't meet the man until just after sunrise and we haven't had time to discuss his income." The moment she said it, Willow knew she should have corralled her impulsive nature. But the deliberate attack on Daisy's code of honor could not go unchallenged. "From the story her cook told me, my sister refused any part of his money for years."

Ellie's eyebrows jerked upward as if attempting to attach themselves alongside her widow's peak. The insulted gossip would find a way to get back at her.

Willow decided to stay as far away from Ellie as possible while the woman remained in High Plains. She had a legitimate excuse to justify the action. Children to watch.

And skills to learn, she added but vowed Ellie would never hear those words from her lips.

At the moment she needed to salvage a sticky bouquet and ward off any further pests.

"Here, need this?" Gage handed Willow a cloth napkin he'd borrowed when she'd backed up and plowed the bouquet into the side of the cake. "I dipped it in the lake and thought you could use it."

Her cheeks turned rosy as she accepted the cloth and held the flowers out to him. "Will you hold these while I wipe my hands? I seem to be an accident waiting to happen lately."

He accepted the bouquet, noticing the icing-laced flowers had destroyed its beauty. "Tell you what— why don't we replace the bad clusters with some good ones? There are plenty of fresh ones to pick along the slope. No one will ever notice the difference."

"You wouldn't mind helping me?" she asked, staring at the ribbons of lace that held the clusters together. "You think we can make it look presentable?"

"It would be my pleasure to help. Just walk over and moisten the cloth again, then join me," he instructed. Picking flowers wasn't exactly one of his better skills, but one she seemed to need at the moment. How hard could gathering flowers be? "We'll need something clean to wipe our hands with when we're done."

While she did as he suggested, Gage quickly unknotted the lace tied around the stems and took the bouquet apart. He separated good from bad and dropped the ruined clusters into one of the empty barrels near the tables.

Remembering his mission, he squinted hard at the crowd, looking at each male face again for sign of the horse thief among them. Not so far that he could see. Trouble was, the guests seemed countless and the pesky Texas sun was shining so bright it hurt his eyes to stare too long at their features.

"Is something wrong?" Willow asked as she returned. "Have you changed your mind?"

He shook his head. "Let's head this way."

They moved uphill against the tide of visitors flooding the area. "That patch looks healthy," he said, bending down to pick a cluster and adding it to the bouquet. Ants immediately crawled up his fingers and he shook them off, not wanting her to notice. They'd been stirred up by last night's rainstorm and were on the march. He hoped the ladies were keeping close watch on the food tables or they would have a few more diners than they expected.

"Let's go over there," he suggested.

She hurried to match his stride and Gage appreciated that she was long legged enough to keep up with him. Still, he slowed down a little so she wouldn't become winded.

Gage offered his arm and she linked hers through it. After a few steps, they settled into a comfortable pace together.

"I heard Mr. Parker recently bought a large remuda of horses." He mentioned the interesting fact he'd learned since arriving for the ceremony.

"Bass plans to build a barrel factory when he returns from their honeymoon," Willow informed him. "Daisy says wood will have to be hauled here to build and supply the factory and that means he'll need lots of horses to pull wagons. He got a good deal on them at a fort near Mobeetie and even hired a wrangler there to watch them while he and Daisy are away. I met the man last night. Shepard Hutton's his name. My sisters seem to like him well enough."

Shepard Hutton? Stanton Hodge? Just coincidence the two men shared the same initials? Gage took note. Lots of horses meant opportunities for thieves. He wanted to talk with this Hutton fellow up close. If he wasn't the man Gage tracked, then he needed to be warned about the thief being in the area. Nothing more appealing to a rustler than an absentee owner. Like dangling a bone in front of a starving dog and daring him to bite.

Gage bent and picked another cluster of verbena, adding it to the group. She bent with him. No ants this direction. "What do you think? Enough?"

Willow shook her head. "One more ought to do it. From here or somewhere else?"

"Anywhere this direction seems good." He straightened and moved on. "Would you mind pointing out the hired man when we get back? I'd like to let him know if you or your family needs my help while Parker's gone, he can call on me."

"He chose not to come to the wedding," Willow said. "Even though Bass hired a few extra wranglers to relieve him for a couple of hours, Shepard said it was his job to make sure all the teams and buggies were taken care of. I'm glad he's so dedicated to his job. He's keeping the horses in the back pasture so the manure will be downwind of the guests."

She laughed and Gage liked this more relaxed view of Willow. When she smiled, he thought he even noticed a few freckles sprinkled across her nose. Blinking away the sunlight for a moment to refocus, he stared intently and was pleased to see he hadn't been wrong. Freckles. They fit her well.

His eyes locked with her Palomino-colored gaze and he thought he'd just witnessed the most frightening sight he'd ever seen. A glimmer of a future that might have been but would never be his.

Gage glanced behind them and noticed Myrtle stood near the tables and lifted a triangle of iron in her hands. "We better choose the last cluster and get back. I think we're out of time."

He bent and chose one more bunch and handed them all to Willow.

"Please, you tie them together," she insisted.

As he took the lace ribbon from his pocket and completed the task, Gage kept his thoughts away from her beautiful eyes. *Focus on why you came here today*, he reminded himself.

Shepard Hutton sounded like a man who would do his best to protect the women, children and property put in his charge. That fact appealed to Gage and reassured him that he could bide time until after the newlyweds were on their way before warning the wrangler of Hodge's presence in the community.

Maybe there would still be time to have one final word with Bass and suggest that he keep the extra hired men after the wedding as a safety precaution. That way, the men could ride for the brand and Hutton wouldn't be out here on his own.

Every instinct inside Gage warned this was just the kind of situation the thief thrived in taking advantage of. Gage would count himself no kind of lawman if he didn't warn everyone that their choices had put them in jeopardy.

Parker might be rich enough to take a loss as most couldn't, but Gage didn't want him to be so in love at the moment that he unknowingly put his children and sisters-in-law at risk.

Snow and the skillet-wielding cook probably had a few tricks under their bonnets to fend off trespassers. And he wouldn't put it past the children to give Hodge a good deal of frustration. But from what he'd learned of Willow so far, she might be an easy hostage.

The sound of iron clanging the triangle signaled all that it was time to mosey on in and commence to eating.

But it sounded more like a bell of warning.

Willow hadn't proven herself capable of evading any kind of trouble yet.

Chapter Six

Pride filled Willow as she watched Daisy stand in the two-seated buggy decorated with white lace ribbons and a Just Married banner strung along its back. As her sister turned to toss the bouquet into the air, Willow considered her mission finally accomplished. She'd managed to deliver the flowers safely into the bride's hands without any further trouble.

The sweet verbena sailed high above the group of eligible women vying to catch the prospect of being next in line to wed.

Suddenly, Willow realized the bouquet was headed straight for her. Marriage was the last thing she had on her mind. She dodged as other women nearly knocked her down to reach for it. She stumbled, attempting to remain upright.

"Pardon me," she said but only managed to collide the crinoline hoops beneath her dress against theirs, making them all look as if they were human bells set into sway. The bouquet bounced off Willow's right shoulder and shattered apart, showering the contenders with pink petals. The lace she and Gage had tied to bind the flowers together had not held.

Disappointment echoed among the would-be brides and Willow received a few glares that assured her some of them blamed her for not getting out of the way fast enough.

A strong hand grabbed her arm and laced it through his more muscular one, stopping her from swaying and pulling her closer.

"Wave to your sister, Willow," Gage's voice instructed. "She'll never really know what happened until she gets back, and only if you decide to tell her. Right now let her be happy to be on her way."

The crowd cheered and shouted their blessings as the buggy pulled away and the newlyweds headed to whereabouts known only to them for the next two months.

Willow leaned into Gage slightly, appreciating his calm logic. Most likely, her sister thought the bouquet had burst apart simply because of where it had bounced from, not for any other reason. But Willow knew she had only dodged blame this time.

Now she had to find a way to make it up to the women who'd lost out on catching the bouquet. Add that to her ever-growing list of must-dos.

"Why don't we see how I can help get you done here with your guests? I'd like to catch the Trumbo brothers and maybe talk to your horse wrangler after he's done seeing that everybody's got their teams."

"I was told to make sure my niece and nephew don't get underfoot while our cook and my sister take care of the cleanup. Snow said she and the towns-women will wash dishes near the lake and those of the men who care to help can tote everything back to the house. Myrtle will make sure the men stack everything back exactly where it belongs."

Gage laughed. "She sounds like she could command an army."

"I don't know her well enough yet to say, but those children seem to respect her," Willow admitted.

"So, how can I help?" Gage offered again. "You want me to tote?"

"How about you and I prepare a basket of food for Shepard and his helpers? They should be ready to eat after all the teams are gone. Myrtle really didn't have time to cook breakfast for the men this morn-ing, with all of this to do. I'm sure the children will want to go along with us. Ollie especially. She won't want Snow to put her to work doing dishes."

Willow slipped her arm away from Gage's and headed toward the food tables, calling her niece and nephew to join her there. They approached warily, as if they suspected chores would now commence. She grinned, hoping to reassure them that she had something more fun in mind to occupy them.

When Willow told the pair what she and Gage

had planned, their eyes lit up and they started loading two empty baskets.

"You think Shepard will like cinnamon rolls?" Ollie asked. She took a bite, then put the remainder into her basket. "Or maybe this one. It's got some kind of berries in it. I forget what they're called."

She took a bite and spat it out, tucking it next to the last partial. "Yuck, not me. Maybe he'll eat the rest. Mama says don't be wasteful."

"He likes meat." Thad forked pieces of ham and beefsteak into a cloth napkin and wrapped them up. "Told me once the only thing he don't eat is horseflesh."

"Put enough in for four men, not just Shepard," Willow reminded, adding several biscuits and boiled eggs to each child's basket. "They'll be hungry."

Gage moved close to Thaddeus. "Mind if I help?"

Thaddeus's chin lifted as the boy stared up at Willow's tall guest. "Okay. Just get four of everything and put it in thisaway."

The child was apparently precise about how he did things. Willow was a bit envious. Thad was fortunate to master that skill at such a young age.

She noticed Gage squinting as he studied the inside of the basket before placing the food he'd gathered there. Was he placating her nephew or had the sun made it hard for him to spot the boy's pattern? He seemed pretty patient with Thaddeus. Kind to children. He rose a notch in her estimation of him.

Gage glanced up and his eyes met hers.

Not wanting him to think she'd been watching,

she averted her gaze and focused on helping Ollie finish their basket.

"We're done," Ollie announced. "We beat y'all."

"Nuh-uh," Thad challenged. "We was already done. I just didn't say it."

They argued back and forth a minute until Gage finally spoke up. "It was a tie."

Both children instantly clammed up. Willow marveled that a simple tone of voice had an effect as powerful as if he'd aimed a gun at them or given an order. Yet he hadn't. Gage had only made a statement that dared anyone to challenge what he said.

Ooh, she could definitely use that in her notes for future reference. A Ranger would know how to use his voice in such a bold manner. So would an outlaw, for that matter.

She, too, needed a chance to talk with Shepard Hutton.

Maybe he knew more about Gage Newcomb and what the man did for a living.

Surely it wouldn't hurt asking him about it.

As he, Willow and the children approached Daisy Parker's homestead, Gage blinked hard and peered at one man holding a team of horses still while his coworker helped visitors claim and board the appropriate wagon or buggy. When one wagon departed the dusty path that separated the main house from the corral and barn, the second pair of workers prepared the same for the next group ready to leave. Shepard and his helpers worked with precision.

The top hand knew his job well.

Gage had spotted the boss among them purely by how the other three waited on a nod of approval from Shepard before moving from one position to hurry on to the next. He'd almost missed that nod, the sun so bright and high in the sky, but Gage kept staring long enough. Hard enough. He finally caught it.

The top hand wasn't the biggest built or the tallest among the men, but the rowels on his spurs chinked the loudest when he walked. Gage found himself listening harder lately, realizing that sound was a friend he relied on now.

The four workmen wore bandannas across their noses, looking like bandits sizing up the teams. Gage figured the kerchiefs helped relieve the men from sucking in dirt stirred up beneath the horse's hooves as they jolted into action.

It must have been a long morning for each man, riding herd on so many horses and keeping the smell away from the festivities. Their efforts had served the wedding well. The sweet scent of verbena and mounds of delicious food had enhanced the serene atmosphere.

No telling when Shepard and his men would be finished and able to eat, since people were still helping with the cleanup. Gage didn't envy them, but he admired a man who stayed the course when doing a job. It showed a code of honor and grit. He approved of the chosen hired hand the more he noticed about him.

"Want me to call Shepard over?" Willow asked as they finally reached the house and stopped to rest from their long walk.

"I'll get him for you," Ollie offered, setting her basket down to get a head start on her brother.

"I will, too." Thaddeus thrust his basket into Gage's hand.

"Both of you stay here," Willow demanded. "I don't want either of you underfoot. There's too many horses. As fast as the wagons are getting under way, you'll get hurt. Stay with Mr. Newcomb for a minute. I'll ask him to come."

Before either could protest or Gage could discourage her, Willow headed toward Hutton. The man looked up as she awkwardly danced and dodged around the horses to reach him.

Gage got a better glimpse of the wrangler's features. Black hair, average nose, eyes a color he couldn't define well in this sunlight. It was hard to tell if the man wore a mustache or beard since a bandanna covered that part of his face.

Something in Hutton's features changed the more Willow talked to him. He stared once at Gage, then back at her and shook his head. Gage couldn't help but wonder what she had said to him. Maybe the man was upset with having to stop his job and come greet a stranger. Not that Gage could blame him. He didn't like to be disturbed either when he was taking care of business.

Finally, Hutton shrugged, Willow turned, and both headed toward Gage. Gage decided he'd make this talk short. No need to irritate him further.

The *chink, chink, chink* of Shepard's spurs announced their approach.

He didn't stop close. Near enough to be polite but far enough away to keep a reserved distance.

The sun was behind the ranch hand, making it difficult for Gage to see much more than he'd already noticed.

"Gage, this is Shepard Hutton," Willow said. "Shepard, Gage Newcomb."

Hutton tipped his hat slightly, not extending his hand to shake. The hat came to rest lower on his forehead, taking away even more of Gage's view.

"Boss here says you wanted to talk to me about something." His muffled voice sounded impatient. He glanced back at his men and frowned as the next team in line stalled.

"Let's give the kids a break. They've been working pretty hard bringing food for you and your men." Gage shared a glance with Willow. No need to frighten the children. Hopefully, she would get the message and send them off to play so he and Shepard could discuss this business freely.

She took his hint. "Okay, kids, take a minute or two but stay away from where they're loading the teams."

The children cheered and challenged each other to race to the salt shed and back.

As soon as they were off, Gage said to the top hand, "I need to talk to you about horse thieves."

"What about them?"

Willow looked surprised. "You didn't say anything about horse thieves. Just that you wanted to offer him your help if he needs it."

"There's a dangerous one in the vicinity. Maybe more," Gage said, knowing that preparing her for a threat was the best way to protect her from harm. His attention switched back to the wrangler. "Thought I'd give you a warning so you can be on the lookout for trouble."

"What's he look like?" Hutton asked.

Gage shared the thief's description. "About your height, I'm guessing. He's usually on horseback when I've seen him, so I'm not sure exactly how tall he is. Red haired. Has a gold tooth."

"Wanted by the law?"

"So I've heard." Gage had learned not to reveal more than was necessary until he'd sized up a man completely. He'd give Hutton time to prove himself worth trusting.

"Ain't seen any thieves around here." Hutton's head turned as laughter came rushing by. "Just kids."

The children chose that moment to return and chased each other between the adults, arguing about which of them would now be thief and the other sheriff in their ongoing pursuit, which took them away again.

"You the law?" Hutton faced him again.

Gage noted that the man's voice held no particular regard for authority. Not uncommon with men who worked the circuit of ranches who needed spring and summer help. Respect was bought and paid for by the highest wage.

Willow stared at Gage intently, and he had a pretty good idea why she might be interested in the answer he'd give.

"You might say I come from a long line of lawmen," Gage told the man.

"Thanks for the warning." Hutton turned abruptly to call back over his shoulder as he walked off, "I'll make sure to look for signs of trouble."

Something about the top hand left Gage unsettled. This one meeting wasn't enough to assure him that Willow and her family would be safe under the wrangler's care. Gut instinct told Gage to watch and wait before he trusted.

But the clock was ticking and watching was no longer his best skill.

Waiting had become his only fear.

A *whoosh, whoosh, whoosh* jerked Gage from his thoughts as a long black stretch of leather rent the air and struck near the feet of the stalled team. Hair rose on the back of his neck as the whip recoiled and returned into the gloved palm of its masterful handler.

Hutton.

Gage had forgotten to add one fact in the description he'd shared with the top hand.

The thief had a way with a whip.

Chapter Seven

All but one of the guests had long departed. The wranglers were in the barn taking a well-deserved break from chores and finally getting to eat. The dishes and house had been put back in Myrtle's required order, and the children were champing at the bit to go into town.

The family members left behind sat in the parlor with their remaining guest, Gage Newcomb. Willow suspected he lingered there so he'd get another chance to talk with Shepard but was being polite enough to wait and let the man eat his food.

Why hadn't he talked to her about the possibilities of horse thieves in the area? Did he think only the men needed to know? If so, she wasn't sure she liked that about Gage. Did he think women were too delicate to handle bad news? She'd have to learn the answer to that question when they were alone practicing the skills he planned to teach her.

She wondered what he'd say if she mentioned that Shepard happened to have a gold tooth. Who would he trust then? She didn't want him talking to their hired hand again until she had a chance to find out why Shepard hadn't mentioned that fact to Gage. If she planned to be a reporter someday, she needed to test her skill at gathering information discreetly.

"Why do you want to go to town?" Willow asked her niece and nephew, switching her attention to the children. She hoped to guide the conversation into a way she could spend some time in town this afternoon. "Haven't you had enough of visiting this morning?"

"Shepard's supposed to fetch Mama and Daddy's buggy from the livery," Ollie said, fidgeting in her ladder-back chair and squirming in her frilly dress. "They're gonna leave it with Bear after they catch the stage. That means he'll have room to bring us back, too."

"He can't take a wagon to pick up a buggy," Willow reasoned. If they did go, she'd have to let the child change clothes. The little tomboy disliked being in anything but overalls.

"How did you two plan on getting there?" Gage asked.

Willow wondered the same thing. If she managed this just right, if she could somehow go along, this might give her the perfect opportunity to make things right with Bear and maybe even a few of the women she'd bumped into during the bid for the bouquet. Bouquet tossing should not be that dangerous!

Both children stared at Gage as if he'd asked something even a five-year-old would know the answer to. Her niece's eyes disappeared into a forest of lashes as she said, "Shepard will ride his horse and I'll sit behind him."

"I'll sit in front," Thaddeus spoke up for himself, thumbing his suspenders with a pop to show he meant business.

Not to be outdone, Ollie continued, "When we head home, he'll just tie his horse to the back of the buggy and—" she raised her palms in the air "—there we go!"

"How about I ride along beside you," Gage suggested, "then one of you can ride with me?"

"Yay!" the children chimed in unison.

Willow shook her head, even though she saw Gage's real purpose for offering. She didn't want him and Shepard talking about thieves in front of the children. "Let Shepard and his men rest until we get back. Snow and Myrtle could use some time to themselves, too. I'll ride with you and the children, and I'll bring the buggy home."

Enlisting the children's enthusiasm, Willow asked, "You don't mind showing me the town a bit, do you?"

Ollie and Thad shared a conspiratorial look and shook their heads.

"I'll show ya just everythin'." Ollie grinned.

"More than you wanna see, prob'ly," Thad replied, his sandy-colored eyebrows rising and lowering as though they were blankets offering some kind of smoke signal.

Willow had a feeling her niece had plans of her own in town and her brother didn't want to be too much of a snitch. Yet he was trying to give her a hint. She'd expected some kind of challenge from the children, so it didn't surprise her that she would need to tread cautiously with the pair.

Duly warned, she returned her attention to Snow and Myrtle. "I have a few things I need to take care of in town and I'd really enjoy taking the kids off your…uh… Spending some time alone with them."

She kind of meant it. Willow had to see how well she could handle them on her own.

"I told Shepard we could wait until tomorrow to pick up the buggy." Snow exhaled a long breath as she rubbed the back of her neck and moved closer to Willow.

"Let her go if she wants," Myrtle insisted. "Don't know about you, but I could use a nap."

The cook yawned so wide the children laughed.

"We've got enough food left over," Myrtle continued. "I don't have to fix anything for a couple of meals. You ought to take your sister up on the offer, Snow, and get some rest yourself."

Snow bent down and leaned closer to Willow's ear, the fragrance of the orange groves back home in Florida ever a part of her presence. Did her sister still take the time to make her own perfume? Willow wondered.

"Are you sure you want to do this?" Snow whispered. "Remember that time you got lost and had to ride out the hurricane all by yourself? You were so scared, being alone. What about when the team got away from you and—?"

"I won't be alone," Willow answered softly, trying to hold back her resentment of being reminded of the times she'd failed miserably to prove herself capable.

"Ollie and Thad are a handful under the best of conditions. I should go with you," Snow insisted.

Willow turned and studied her, deciding if she didn't stand her ground here and now, they would be testing each other's will the entire time Daisy was gone. Even though Willow understood that her sister *meant* to be protective, Snow always made her feel like an egg that had cracked too early in the henhouse. Too fragile to live.

"That won't be necessary." Willow met her eye to eye, standing from the settee across from the children. "Thank you for offering, sis, but you're worrying needlessly."

"Then it's settled." Gage stood and moved to retrieve his hat from the rack near the door. "I'll tell Mr. Hutton you're taking care of this and have him saddle you a horse. That'll give you a few minutes to get ready."

"No need," Willow said, watching Snow's mouth straighten into a hard line of disapproval as she headed toward the stairs. Was she so angry that she wasn't going to see them off?

"Ollie, come upstairs and change into your overalls. No need to mess up that dress," Snow ordered as she headed toward the second-story landing. "Thad, do you plan on wearing those or are you changing?"

The boy snapped the suspenders that held up his pants and left his black string tie on. "What I'm wearing suits me. Makes me look brand-new."

It took everything Willow had to ignore Snow's commands to the children to prove she still held the reins of authority. She couldn't blame her sister. Until today Willow had thought she deserved most of what Snow felt about her. She just needed to start somewhere with showing Snow that she was different from before and meant to prove herself more than capable of being left in charge. There was no better time to prove it than today. Right now.

"Okay, then, if you're already dressed, Thad, go see that Shepard saddles me a horse." Willow shooed the boy out of the door. "Tell him what we're doing and that we'll be back before nightfall. Also let him know that he and his men have the rest of the afternoon off, and we really appreciate all the hard work they've done today."

"I'll try and remember all that," Thaddeus said and raced toward the barn.

About fifteen minutes later, Gage and the children were saddled and waiting out front. Willow had written down the names of the women included in the crush of the bridal bouquet and had a fairly good idea of where she might find those who lived in town. Myrtle told her if she couldn't remember, the blacksmith or his wife might be willing to help her find them.

"Mind yourself and those children," the cook said, standing at the door to wave them off. "And Snow will get over her snit with you."

As Willow made her way down the porch steps, the salt-and-pepper-haired woman hollered past her, "Be nice, you two, or you won't get to go with your aunt again."

"Yes, ma'am," they echoed in unison, waving back.

Willow faced Myrtle. "Tell Snow not to worry. I'll bring them back safely."

"It's not them she's worried about, honey. Those two could find their way back like two pigeons looking for home. It's *you* she's worried about. She's just tired. I told her I'd see you all off."

"Thank you," Willow said and headed down the steps to be on her way. She hadn't wanted to quarrel with Snow at all, and it hurt her feelings that Snow didn't want to wave goodbye. Maybe she'd be in a better humor once they returned and she'd rested up.

Half expecting Gage to be waiting beside her horse to help her mount, Willow was surprised to find him sitting behind Thaddeus, looming tall in the saddle.

She hoped he was better at skills than showing

good manners. Feeling slighted, she grabbed the reins, sticking her heel in one stirrup to swing a leg over and rest herself firmly in her saddle behind Ollie. She hadn't hired him for his manners, after all.

"Good," Gage complimented her. "You did that fairly well. Now let's see how well you ride."

He commanded his horse into action and headed down the path to town.

He'd been testing her, purposely waiting to see if she could mount properly. Her grandfather had taught her *some* things already. She wasn't completely ignorant of the ways of the West. Horseback riding was one of her favorite childhood experiences, and Grandfather had enjoyed teaching her how to handle a horse properly.

Willow wrapped one arm around Ollie's waist to make sure her niece was secure and took off at a gallop to catch up.

"Better slow down some," Gage shouted as she swept past him. "He might pull a shoe."

Logic echoed in his warning. It sounded as if her grandfather could have been saying the same thing. Willow slowed the horse's gait to a trot, not wanting to put Ollie or their mount in any danger.

"Glad you're wise enough not to let anger get the best of you," Gage said as he and the boy moved up alongside them and settled into an even pace. "That shows good sense."

She only half heard his approval. "What do you mean? I wasn't angry."

"Sure you were, Aunt Willow," Ollie agreed. "Your arm heated up and gripped me so hard all a sudden that I thought you was tryin' to crack me like a pecan shell. You got mad, all right."

Gage laughed. Thaddeus glanced at Willow as if he was waiting to see how she would take Ollie's defense of Gage. Not wanting to make her nephew feel cautious about being himself around her or contradict what her niece had clearly discerned, Willow gave in and smiled. "I guess I was at that."

Thaddeus erupted into one of the sweetest laughs she had ever heard. Willow immediately wondered if he was someone like her—careful not to say or do anything unless certain it wouldn't offend anyone or make her appear foolish. Her heart went out to him if they shared such a habit and she decided she'd see if she could help him gain some confidence while she was here.

Silence rode with them awhile until Gage finally spoke up. "I take it you didn't want me discussing anything further with Mr. Hutton."

"Little ears have big imaginations," she replied. "No reason that couldn't wait until another time."

"That means she didn't want us to hear what you and Shepard woulda said," Thaddeus explained.

"Besides, Aunt Willow had to go. She's got plans once we get there," Ollie added. "I heard her talking with Myrtle about all them ladies she's gonna find."

"Like I said," Willow told him, "little ears have big imaginations. I'm just going to check on the livery and set things right there. Then I plan to make myself better acquainted with the town. Nothing wrong with that, is there?"

Gage took his attention away from the pathway for a moment, facing her and letting his horse have its rein. "When do we start your first lesson?"

"Lesson?" Ollie hollered. "We ain't goin' to do no lessons until school starts, are we? If we start now we'd been in real danger of overlearnin' something."

Willow glared at Gage, wishing he hadn't brought up the subject of the lessons, but she couldn't blame him. She hadn't asked him not to mention them to anyone. Another thing to add to her list of must-dos. Come up with a logical reason why she'd enlisted his help. Maybe the truth would serve her well. She could just say she wanted to learn how to be a Texan quicker and he'd agreed to offer some lessons.

Then again, maybe Ollie would forget about it without asking more. "No lessons or school for you until it takes up session again, sweetie."

Ollie squealed. "That's good. Don't remind Aunt Snow. She'll think up some homework to get us primed up."

"Well, I wish it was already time to start school," Thad informed them.

"That's 'cause you need to get smarter," Ollie retaliated, sticking out her tongue. "I'm smarter than an old hoot owl. Just ask anybody."

Willow listened to them banter back and forth about who had outwitted whom recently. The fact that they would be in school for hours each day soon would give her extra time to meet with Gage without affecting her responsibility with them.

The road suddenly forked in two directions. The children were arguing so loudly Willow could hardly concentrate. She wasn't sure which way was the correct road to High Plains, so she just reined to a halt. Waiting on Gage to start down the right path, she was surprised when he reined up short beside her.

"Time to see if you can follow trail," Gage announced. "Which way?"

The children quit arguing and started to point the direction, but Gage's command stopped them. "No, let her figure it out for herself. She needs to know how to get back and forth from town to home on her own."

Panic rose within Willow. What if she got it wrong and made a fool of herself in front of the children? She thought the lessons would be learned in front of him, not everybody. Maybe she needed to add a few rules to the lessons.

Willow frowned at Gage.

"Can we give her a hint?" Thaddeus asked as if he thought she was struggling.

She wanted to slap that expression of infinite patience right off Gage's face when he shook his head and said, "What if nobody was here to give her one?"

He glared at the bright sun and blinked hard. "Never know when you need to rely on all your own senses. Let's see what your aunt can do."

Willow took a hard look at her surroundings. The sun shone slightly past midway in the sky, so that meant it was just past noon. It would set in the west, of course, and High Plains faced east. She thought she caught a white plume of smoke rising in the distance, which could be from someone's chimney or maybe the diner in town. It made sense that the right part of the fork would lead them to High Plains.

But she wanted to make certain of her choice. A quick study of the wagon ruts leading in that same direction showed heavier grooves and cut a clear path of nothing but well-trodden dirt that had known many travelers. The fork to the left still grew clumps of prairie grass along the way.

Pleased with her deductions, Willow chose the path to the right and said, "We're headed this way."

"Mighty fine," Gage complimented her, joining in beside her. "You didn't rush your decision and that's what counts when figuring out a smart move. Tell me why you chose the right."

She gave him all her reasons.

"And when you head back, which way is home?"

"I'll turn left."

"I'd give you an A on this."

Willow was pleased with herself and even happier that his compliment sounded sincere.

Who knew? Maybe she was smarter than she or any of Biven's readers thought she might be.

Maybe all she needed was to think things through more thoroughly before applying them to her stories.

Hopefully, time would tell.

Or rather, one month of lessons would provide.

Her reply to the letter she received from her boss last night rested in her pocket. He wanted to review her first story one month from yesterday. Mailing took a week or more at best, longer if there were problems along the route. That meant she'd have to mail it no later than mid-June in order for it to arrive by the deadline he'd given. Everything had to be sped up twice as fast. The lessons had to be learned quickly. Her help with the children needed to go as flawlessly as possible so she could concentrate well on her writing.

She'd thought she'd have two months before she would be faced with proving herself to Biven.

But now she knew the real challenge would be proving to herself she could do this.

Chapter Eight

When they came to a halt outside the livery, Gage noticed the Trumbo brothers had already begun the repair. Burnt wood had been stripped from inside and now lay in a stack near the door, which was propped open by a wagon wheel. Fresh planks leaned against the livery, ready for use. The sound of hammering echoed in rhythm as the three men worked in unison.

Though he hadn't expected them to start until tomorrow, Gage appreciated that they'd chosen not to put it off. He was glad he'd told Willow about his arrangements with the Trumbos. Otherwise, Willow might have taken up the chore herself. He admired her for wanting to set things right, but from what he'd seen so far, she needed a little more experience between wanting and getting done.

Several horses tied to the hitching rail near the trough danced sideways each time the hammers struck. Chickens squawked on a number of make-shift perches around the livery yard, and from the sound of neighs, the blacksmith or carpenters had tied off other horses around back. The building had been emptied of livestock.

"Maybe you ought to go about your other plans until the men finish," Gage suggested. "Then you can come back here and take care of whatever you had in mind for Bear."

He wanted to clear his own saddle first and offer her a hand down, but he had to make sure Willow could dismount as well as she'd taken *to* the saddle. If she met with trouble out on the range, she would need to be good at both mounting and dismounting.

"I'm doing this first," she said, ignoring his advice. "I can carry boards or give the horses a good brushing while they're out here. That'll keep them calm until the hammering stops."

Gage offered Thaddeus a hand, then dismounted while Ollie nearly flew out of the saddle and ran inside.

"What about those two? They could get in the way—" he nodded toward the boy chasing his sister "—or maybe hurt."

"They know horses better than I do, according to my sisters." Willow shook her head, setting her curls afire with light. "They'll be a big help."

He peered harder, wondering what the color of such curls would look like at dawn when the light took on its morning glory and his eyes had rested for the night. He could see so much better then.

Gage shook off his thoughts and reminded himself

that there was no point in wasting time on such wondering. Appreciating the color of a woman's hair was a skill he was losing with no way to get it back. Capturing Stanton Hodge gave him no time to chase matters that would be of little consequence to his future.

All of a sudden, the hammering halted. Gage listened as each man took time and boomed a greeting to the children.

"Hey, what happened to that frilly, flouncy thing you was wearin' this mornin', little britches?"

"Skinned out of it soon as I could, Uncle Mad," Ollie answered.

Though he hadn't been around all that many children in his years on the trail, there was something Gage liked about Ollie. He couldn't remember a time, other than today, when he'd seen the little tomboy in anything but her overalls. Ollie Trumbo was a piece of work and didn't let anybody's opinion stop her from being her own person. If her aunt stuck around High Plains awhile, Willow would learn a thing or two about confidence from the little girl.

"Snow let you come into town already?" asked one of the other uncles.

"I figured we wouldn't get to see you two till Daisy came home," the slightly younger third uncle piped in.

"Aunt Willow brung us. She didn't know no better," Thaddeus informed them with a sudden squeal. "Oww! Don't kick me."

Images of the feisty brother and sister scuffling

urged Gage to finish tying off the reins to secure his horse.

"Better get in there," Willow insisted, forgetting to hitch her horse to the rail. Rushing to lift a plank, she managed to slant it sideways in order to carry the wood more easily.

In trying to keep its weight balanced, she didn't judge the distance between her and Gage and almost slammed the length of it into his stomach. He jumped backward just enough to dodge the edge of the board.

She turned and flashed him a quirk of an eyebrow. "You coming?"

"Right behind you," he answered, leaving out the fact that she'd nearly gutted him. Instead, he took her horse's reins and tied them off, then grabbed a plank, making sure he gave Willow plenty of room to carry hers.

Once inside, he waited until she set the wood down, then did the same with his.

The tallest of the brothers now had Ollie straddled across his right shoulder and the battling children separated. "Glad you could get to town, Willow. Soon as we're done here, I'll buy you and these two kicking mules some ice cream. We're just about finished anyway."

Gage watched as each Trumbo held out a powerful hand and offered her a shake. To his surprise, she firmly shook each instead of curtsying. She seemed to know the brothers well. Obviously old friends from the past.

"It's wonderful to see you, Maddox. You, too, Grissom. Jonas. I was so busy this morning at the wedding I didn't get to visit with any of you much." Willow smiled. "Mr. Newcomb here told me about the arrangements he made with you. I really appreciate you getting to it so fast. Where's Bear?"

"Inside with his wife. We told him we didn't need any help. Almost done. Probably won't even have to use those boards you carried in."

Gage noticed the expression that rippled across her face and wondered if it was disappointment in not being needed. When it came to helping, being kind enough to make the offer was what really mattered. Sometimes people didn't want help. But Willow apparently hadn't learned how to take things in stride.

"We came to take the buggy back home for Daisy, but I have other things I'd like to do before we go." She pulled out a list of names from her skirt pocket. "I hope to pay a call on these women."

Six-foot-five Maddox looked down his broken-in-several-places nose at the list and laughed. "You still like to rattle bones, don't you, gal? I remember at Oktoberfest when you tangled knees and noggins with Mary Lou Lassiter trying to fish that juicy orange out of the dunking tank. You couldn't have been more than six or seven, barely able to lean over the tank of apples, much less see where the orange floated."

His gray eyes lit with amusement. "And best of all, you'd just lost your two front teeth, remember? Once you grabbed hold of that orange, you clamped your jaw shut like a Florida gator and wouldn't let go for nobody's business. Mary Lou fought hard with ya, but you hung on. You still smelled like marmalade when your new teeth grew in."

The younger Trumbo brothers laughed.

Willow apparently didn't think the memory was so hilarious. Gage watched her jam the list back into her pocket and her shoulders set ramrod straight. She might be almost red haired, but there was nothing almost about her temper.

"We all tested our wings at that age and skinned a few knees," Gage defended her, trying to soothe the situation. "Nobody's perfect."

Maddox studied him as if he'd just noticed Gage's presence. "Just warning Willow some of these women ain't gonna have nothin' to do with her for a few change of bonnets. She got 'em all fired up when she made 'em miss catching that bachelor snatcher this morning. They'll stay mad till somebody else sets them to cacklin'."

"Got any idea where she'll find the ladies right now?" Gage wanted to make sure she at least got a try at whatever she had in mind.

"Over at the diner." Maddox wiped the sweat from his brow with an arm that looked as if it had been carved from a band of iron railing. "Last I heard, they're having a hen party, sharing notes about the strutting roosters at the wedding. Most of us unmarried fellas are steerin' clear and makin' ourselves plenty useful elsewhere. If Ollie and Thad want ice cream, I'll pull up my bootstraps and test the rapids if I have to. But you might want to stay clear, Newcomb. I hear tell they think you're prime pickings."

Gage knew Maddox was either acting as a big brother to Willow or telling him to stay out of his business where she was concerned. Had there been any courting between the pair in the past? He figured the giant would have been more interested in one of the older sisters. Snow, maybe, since Daisy's affections belonged to Parker.

Gage had known his fair share of fights. He wouldn't want to anger Maddox, or any of his brothers, for that matter. They had a reputation for putting men in their places, but so did he. Gage respected men who set their boundaries and tolerated no interference. But he wouldn't back off from a run-in with them or let any of them shake Willow's confidence in what she meant to do. If she intended to go to the diner, he'd walk her there himself. Whether Maddox approved or not.

Still, he wouldn't make himself a target to an eager group of aspiring brides. They were looking out for their futures. Something they thought he could offer.

"You ready to head that way?" Gage lent his arm so that she would link hers with his. "We'll catch as many of the women as we can now and grab the buggy later."

"Children, come with me, please. Ice cream

sounds nice right about now." She allowed him to escort her out of the building and across the street.

Several people walking along the sidewalks greeted Gage with smiles or friendly nods of acknowledgment as they passed. He didn't miss how pride seemed to fill Willow.

Hammering resumed behind them while Ollie and Thaddeus ran past, each racing to reach the destination first.

"Wait!" Willow pointed toward the mercantile. "I need to stop in there before we go to the diner. It won't take but a minute or two."

"Aww, do we have to go with ya?" Ollie pleaded. "We can get a seat and already be orderin' if you're only gonna be a couple'a minutes."

Both children started backing toward the diner, looking ready to race there at the first sign of approval from their aunt. They reminded Gage of spring colts ready to gallop across open pasture.

Willow glanced at him as if silently asking whether or not he trusted the pair to do what they said they would. He shrugged.

"Your call," he said.

"You're a big help." She frowned.

"Only about things I know. Kids are not in my range of experience," he admitted.

"And you think they're in mine?" Her frown deepened.

"Who knows?" He laughed. "Maybe we'll both

learn something about them while they're in your care."

He'd agreed to teach her skills, not spend his time making sure two adventuresome eight-year-olds kept their promises.

"Okay," she finally relented, "but go nowhere else. Don't order my ice cream, please. I like mine really cold."

The children raced away.

Gage had seen fear shadow anger too often in his lifetime of chasing outlaws. Willow was nervous about something, wanting to pick a fight, and it didn't concern letting the children have their way. What was scaring her?

"You want to go with them?" she asked quickly as if her breath kept pace with the children's footsteps. "I won't be but a minute."

Her hand slipped into her pocket and patted around as if she was trying to locate something in its depth. Had she stored her money there? She'd worn no reticule around her wrist as most women did when they came to town to visit businesses and possibly make purchases. Maybe she was just being careful. Whatever her reason for suggesting he leave, Gage wondered if he needed to tread with a little caution here. After all, he still had no clue if she was as innocent as she seemed or had some connection to the horse thief. The likelihood was getting slimmer if his suspicion about Shepard Hutton proved justified.

"I think we ought to give those two time to prove

they can be trusted. I've got something I want to take care of real quick while you're in the mercantile, but I'll be right back. You'll need some help getting the buggy ready before you head home."

Relief washed across her face as she moved up the steps and disappeared into the general store, her hand now clutching what Gage thought might be an envelope.

The image of the blue-and-gray mail sack Junior Pickens kept near the mail slots at the end of his counter came to mind as Gage wondered if she had written a return letter to whoever had sent her the one she'd received yesterday.

If so, what was all the mystery? Why wouldn't she want him to know she was mailing a reply? Was that why she was so nervous? Fearful? Wanting him out of the way? Afraid he'd see the letter and whom it was intended for?

The mailbag would eventually end up with Bear. He could let the blacksmith in on the fact that he worked for the Corps of Rangers and had to have a look at that particular letter. Gage just wanted to make sure it wasn't addressed to Hodge.

But it felt wrong invading her privacy, and his personal code of honor wouldn't let him follow that particular trail no matter what.

Gage let her go about her business and decided he could take the time to check out the Twisted Spur. Maybe Stanton Hodge would be among the influx of visitors in the saloon. Nothing better than a fresh horde of hefty pockets in town to lure a thief out into a crowd.

He hoped Hodge was among the high rollers. If so, he might be able to put his doubt about Willow to rest. Maybe he could finally accept that she was exactly what she appeared—a poor soul who didn't sit any saddle well and needed to learn how.

That would make him and her alike in ways. Losing things each meant to hold on to. Willow, her self-respect. He, his sight. They both, it seemed, had to learn to look at life in a new way now to find some measure of happiness to keep them going.

"That one right there, sir. You see it?" Willow pointed to a stack of white lace handkerchiefs separated by thin paper to keep them clean. She had caught a glimpse of a tiny bouquet of bluebonnets embroidered in one corner of a hankie and hoped there would be several like it—at least one to give each lady concerned.

The choice was the perfect gift to make amends with—delicate, bridal looking and with a hint of flowers. "Exactly how many do you have just like it? I need eight."

The merchant counted and told her. "One more than you want, miss. It'd be a shame to leave just this one."

He was a good salesman, she'd give him that. He left no possible sale undone. Willow admired the lovely lace and decided to purchase the last one for

Daisy. She'd been too focused on escaping Atlanta to think of buying her sister a wedding present. Too bad there were not two extra. She would have offered Snow one, as well.

But then, Snow would probably have considered it some kind of peace offering and that would have taken the pleasure out of giving it.

Lifting the list of ladies' names from her pocket, Willow handed it to the merchant. "You're sure they'll get these tomorrow or the next day?"

The thin man bobbed his head as he pointed to the angled mail slots at the end of his business counter. "I'll wrap them up and put them in the mail before I close up tonight. Most of the ladies check their slots once or twice a week. Those that don't, Bear Funderburg takes their mail out to their ranches. He'll see they get delivered."

"And my letter? When will it go out? When's the next stage?" Her attention swept to the mailbag, which looked much like the one that had ridden with her across country. Would the blacksmith have to sort the bag of letters before hers went on its proper way?

Every step of the process seemed a delay in getting it to Atlanta in time.

"If you'd have brought it to me an hour ago, it could have gone out on the stage with the honeymooners." The merchant's face broadened with a toothsome smile. "Probably didn't think to hand it to your sister, didja?"

"Her mind was busy elsewhere, as you can imagine. I didn't have the heart to bother her with it," Willow said, hoping to make light of her comment. Handing Daisy the letter would only have stirred her sister's curiosity and made her wonder why she hadn't taken up Gage's offer last night to return a reply for her. She would eventually tell Daisy and Snow about what had happened in Atlanta, but hopefully, it would all be resolved before the newlyweds returned.

She wanted it to become just something they all laughed about someday, not another failure to define her.

A scuffle of boots coming up the steps to the mercantile made Willow swing around to find Gage's tall form entering the general store. He'd finished quicker than she had. Hastily, she completed her business with Junior Pickens, snatching the list from his hand. "Remember that I said no one is to know those are from me. I appreciate you keeping my confidence and I'm sure we'll do more business together if you do." She kept her tone low. "Understood?"

Her eyes slanted in Gage's direction. "No one."

"I look forward to doing more business with you, miss." The merchant handed her the extra hankie. "Would you like to have this wrapped, as well—?"

"That's unnecessary," she interrupted, taking Daisy's hankie and stuffing it and the list inside her pocket. She acknowledged Gage's presence in the store a little louder. "I'll spend more time here another day. My friend and I here—" she swung around and motioned to Gage "—have two precocious little children waiting on us over at the diner."

"Your sister's?" asked Junior Pickens. "Ollie and Thaddeus?"

"One and the same." Gage stopped a breath away from the back of Willow's neck. "Actually, that would be two and the same." He laughed. "Never had much of a handle on arithmetic. I like words better."

"You left those kids in the diner on their own?" Junior's eyes widened so fast it looked as if somebody had poked him in the back.

"What's wrong with that?" Willow's head angled toward the direction of the restaurant, then back at the merchant.

Junior studied her. "Nothing. You just might want to make a quick stop over at the bank and set yourself up an account, Miss McMurtry. No telling what those two have ordered. They can outeat an army of starving ants in an empty picnic basket. Better take a bucketful of money with you if you want to leave that fine establishment with your good name and purse intact."

Junior's warning proved all too true. Gage heard Willow groan as she caught sight of her two charges. Ollie and her brother sat at a red-checkered table with bowls of every kind of ice cream imaginable forming a circle in front of each child. A spoonful here and there was missing from the bowls, leaving proof which had been judged the tastiest among the flavors.

Gage would have laughed if he thought he could get away with it. After all, she hadn't told them how much they could order. Just not to order for her.

He thought it was a good time to keep his trap shut and let her do any talking. Sometimes a teacher had best let the student think up the right way to handle something herself.

Thaddeus had loosened his string tie and it now hung as if it were a tongue lapping up the chocolate mound that peaked just below his chin. His tie jostled with every scoop he shoved into his mouth, sending a brown, frosty smear across his once-clean white shirt.

"They're here," Ollie said, looking up as Gage and Willow approached. "Eat faster. She looks mad."

Thaddeus shoveled faster.

Low murmurs and titters echoed across the dining hall, layering the air with social tension. Gage glared at the men, silently daring any one of them to make an open comment against the children or Willow. None seemed to want to challenge him. Several of the women, on the other hand, held their noses and chins at haughty angles that revealed their disapproval of Ollie and Thad's behavior and Willow's lack of control over it.

Ollie's cheeks appeared pinker than usual, or else Gage was just seeing better at the moment. Then he realized strawberry ice cream had sketched clown's lips across the tomboy's face as she'd eaten. She scooted the bowl of strawberry away and started wolfing down a scoop of something that looked as if it might be vanilla topped with blue- or blackberries. He wasn't sure which. Either one would add to the mess when she dug in.

Willow sank slowly into the chair across the table from Thaddeus, not giving Gage time to hold it out for her. Gage took a seat adjacent hers. "Looks like you got a head start on us," he said. "Think we'll join you."

Thaddeus stopped midspoonful, his mouth still gaping to take the next bite. He waited a moment, his attention focusing on Gage's face, then on his aunt's. Finally he asked, "We're not in trouble?"

"Sure we are," Ollie answered, her tongue darting out to lick her top lip free of a blueberry. "Aunt Willow just ain't gonna yell at us here. Prob'ly at home, where Aunt Snow and Myrtie can back her up. I hear 'em all now. 'What do you mean eating all that ice cream?'" Ollie took another bite and nearly purred with pleasure. "But it was sure worth it. Yummm."

Thaddeus looked cautiously at his aunt. "Remember, Aunt Willow, I warned ya about us." He took another bite and licked the spoon. "And there's always no telling what she'll make me do once we get here."

Ollie's sidekick looked sincerely innocent, as if he had been given no say in the matter. The tomboy might prove herself a force to be reckoned with one day. The wish to stick around and see that happen surprised Gage. He couldn't remember a solitary soul he'd ever stayed around to watch grow up. Time and trouble had kept him always on the move.

"That's right. I made him do it," Ollie fessed up. "Couldn't help myself. Just said, 'Ollie, your big brother ain't had much practice in getting in trouble all by hisself, so you better show him how to do it right.'"

Gage lost his composure. He tried not to. He really did, but he couldn't help himself. Thaddeus was right. He had warned Willow. Not exactly in those words, but close enough. And Ollie meant to test her aunt's limits.

Willow would have her hands full in the next few weeks.

Gage started chuckling, that down-deep-in-the-belly amusement that erupts into a blaze of laughter that no problem on earth is big enough, hurtful enough, to extinguish. He snorted, nearly honking like a southbound gander.

The awkwardness he felt at snorting made him laugh even harder...until tears came.

Not the tears from laughing too long.

Tears that sprang from an even deeper well. Unbidden. Unrelenting. Scalding upon the tender flesh that had not yet healed beneath his eyes.

He hadn't spilled them when he'd buried his father beside his dog.

Nor when he learned he was going blind.

Yet here they were. Forming a tide of misery

within him in front of God and strangers alike, and he couldn't control the soul-destroying flood.

For the first time in his life, Gage stood and walked away from someone he meant to help. Willow had to handle this situation on her own.

He was empty.

Void of anything to give.

He had to get out. Away from accepting all he had lost and what he could no longer be.

Willow would have to deal with the ice cream snatchers herself.

Chapter Nine

Willow watched Gage leave and wondered what had just happened. He'd laughed so hard she'd thought he was going to burst at the seams. Then suddenly he'd looked as if he might be crying. Ollie and Thad hadn't been *that* funny. At least, she hadn't thought so, and laughing at the two rascals would only encourage them to do more.

Still, something about his leaving seemed odd. Gage had turned his face away and lit out of the diner as if he were hot on somebody's trail or he'd forgotten something important. Maybe she needed to go see about him.

"I never seen nobody laugh so hard they cried," Thaddeus whispered, pushing away his now empty bowl of chocolate. "You reckon Mr. Newcomb had to go blow his nose or something and didn't want us to watch him do it?"

Ollie looked up from her dessert and laughed.

"Yeah, he probably had some big ol' man boogers, all green and slimy and full of—"

"I think I'm gonna be sick." Thaddeus's skin turned ashen.

"Ollie, you've said enough." Willow closed her eyes to the vivid image her niece had brought to mind. She stood, her stomach roiling. She wouldn't be able to enjoy a single bite of anything, given Ollie's talent for description. Maybe the little mischief maker should become the writer in the family.

When her eyes opened, Willow spotted a few of the women she wanted to make amends with among the diners. No doubt their glares meant she had won none of their approval in the way she'd handled this first outing with her niece and nephew. Maybe it was a good thing she felt so compelled to check on Gage and try to establish a more cordial acquaintanceship with the ladies later.

"Both of you wipe your faces. We're going now," she told the children, motioning for the waitress.

"I'd like to pay our bill, please," she said when a harried-looking woman with a white apron tied around her homespun dress arrived. Of the three servers in the restaurant, this one looked the busiest and seemed unhappy to be called over *yet* again.

"That's fourteen scoops of ice cream," the waitress informed her, checking the order she'd written down. "You sure that's gonna be all this time?"

"Don't forget I had a sarsaparilla," Ollie reminded

her, taking a long drink from the crystal goblet sitting in front of her.

"And one sarsaparilla," the waitress mumbled as she added numbers, then announced, "That'll be one dollar and five cents."

"A dollar five!" Ollie grabbed her napkin and wiped the strawberry ice cream from her lips, then threw it atop one of the empty bowls as she scooted back her chair and stood. "Uh-oh. We may have to wash some dishes if Aunt Willow ain't got that much, Thaddy-Wumpus. You shoulda left that last scoop or two off."

Thaddeus could do nothing but groan as he moved to Willow's side. "I think I'm gonna be sick, Aunt Willow. I can't wash no dishes right now. You got some money, don't ya?"

The waitress flashed Willow a look of concern, but Willow quickly reassured Thad. "No need to wash dishes. I can pay for this. Let's walk with the lady to the register, shall we?"

Willow quickly paid the bill, fortunate that the handkerchiefs had not been all that expensive and she still had the first payment meant for Gage in her pocket. They had not yet established what he would charge, but hopefully, it would be less than whatever she had left once she was done here.

"See those four women sitting at the table together in the corner to the right?" Willow nodded toward the women.

The waitress rattled off their names.

They sounded like names that had been on the list she'd given to the merchant. "Yes, them," Willow said. "How much is their bill altogether?"

After looking through her list of orders, the waitress did some addition, then told Willow the sum.

Willow handed her the money with a generous tip. "That's for theirs and the rest is for you for being so patient with the children. Please don't tell the ladies who did this. Just let it be our little secret, all right?"

"Come back anytime," the waitress said, smiling for the first time since Willow had called her over. She slipped the extra bill into her apron pocket and put the rest into the cash register. "And bring the kids with you, too."

Willow laughed, thinking maybe she'd made herself welcome with at least one person in High Plains. Now she had only a few hundred more to go.

She needed to check the population sign that hung between the doctor's office and undertaker's place of business. It was always good to know exactly how many hurdles one had to jump.

"Hey, look, Aunt Willow." Ollie yanked on her skirt as they stepped out of the diner and onto the planked sidewalk. She pointed toward the livery. "Looks like Uncle Maddox and them are done. All the horses and chickens are back inside, except for Mr. Newcomb's. You reckon that's where he went?"

Surely Gage would have taken his mount with him if he'd gone home, Willow reasoned. But she didn't exactly know where home was for him. He'd never mentioned staying in the boardinghouse or hotel. Never really said anything much about himself, so far. She needed to find him. Pay him for the tracking lesson today. Find out when he could meet with her for the next one. Time was precious.

"Let's go see," she told the children, taking long strides toward the livery. "They must have hitched our horse to the buggy already. One of your uncles might know where Mr. Newcomb went if he's not there."

The town clock that hung just beneath the water tower chimed the hour, reminding Willow that the afternoon was passing quicker than she'd assumed and she needed to finish her business in town. Hopefully, she could still give the horses a good brushdown before she had to keep her word about being home before nightfall.

Much to her surprise, when she entered the livery, the horses were all in their stalls, freshly brushed and curried. The buggy had been stripped of the wedding banner and decorations, and the Trumbos had just finished hitching Daisy's team to it.

"Got it all done for ya," Maddox said, grabbing his hat and signaling his brothers it was time to call it quits.

Willow started to hand them some money but the giant shook his sandy-colored head. "Newcomb already took care of it. We went ahead and put the stock back in their pens and such, brushed 'em down and fed 'em, even told 'em it was a little extra something from you this morning. At least, that's what the man said you'd want them to know. Didn't tell us why. Just said to do it. That right, Newcomb?"

"That's right."

Willow craned her neck to see from where the answer had come and noticed Gage tying the reins of the horse she and Ollie had ridden to the back of the buggy.

"Then we're off," Maddox said. "Come on, boys, and we'll stop in and say howdy to Pigeon before we go. Bear said she wanted to hug on us all and give us a few cookies to take home."

After everyone waved goodbye, Willow returned her attention to Gage. If he had left the diner to hide any pain the tears had inflicted upon his scars, he sure didn't show any now. Maybe he'd just used the situation as an excuse to leave her to her own devices and see how well she handled the predicament with Ollie and Thad.

As he had when he'd shown no manners in helping her mount.

And when he had not guided her way to town.

He hadn't actually taught her anything yet. Just waited to see what she already knew.

And she'd known enough to get them here.

Why had she even bothered worrying about him and his possible pain?

Gage Newcomb was no Texas gentleman, and certainly not one to hitch her wagon to for very long. Not even for lessons she needed to learn.

Why she felt so disappointed in him, she didn't quite understand. It wasn't as if he had to live up to that old list she used to keep about what she expected in a man she might marry. That had been nothing but a twelve-year-old's hero-in-hat-and-buckskin list. They barely knew each other and she hadn't even considered him a possibility for anything other than her tutor.

Had she?

Yet the image of the man she hoped one day might win her heart flashed across her mind. Words that defined him echoed in Willow's ears as if a deep voice whispered them. *Brave. Honest. Challenging. Code of honor. Knows his worth and appreciates yours.*

She rarely allowed herself to think that such a man could ever come into her life. To love her. So she simply told everyone she preferred not to marry.

No man would ever live up to those qualities. She'd set her sights too high. Her would-be hero had been based on everything her grandfather had said *he* had been back in his younger days. She'd learned that was a lie now, or at best, an old man's embellishment of the truth.

Her kind of hero simply didn't exist.

"Y'all about ready to head out?" Gage finally moved around from the back and approached her. "You need to finish up whatever else you have to do and be on your way now."

His face looked carved from stone. Unreadable. Sullen.

What was he angry about? And at whom was

his anger directed? The children? No, he'd laughed at them. The Trumbos? His wave to them seemed friendly enough. Her? What could she have possibly done wrong to deserve such a sour-looking expression?

She wished he weren't right about the lack of time. She'd go hunt up some other capable local willing to show her the way Texans did things well.

"Tell you what, Mr. Newcomb. If you're still interested in earning that money we talked about, show up at the ranch around ten in the morning and I'll be ready and waiting for you. In fact—" Willow reached into her pocket and grabbed the rest of the funds she had with her "—here's a payment for today. I'll pay you by the lesson, since I haven't made up my mind how many I'll require."

He shook his head and didn't reach for the money. "Keep it. Wait till I've earned it. Then you can pay me what I ask. I didn't teach you anything today. You just showed me what you've already got."

At least he's honest, Willow thought, slipping the money back into her pocket.

"Oh, and next time, be sure and remember to hitch or hobble your horse when you mean for him to wait for you," Gage said as his midnight gaze challenged hers. "It's a long walk back wherever you go without him."

Willow started to object, wondering why he was spoiling for a fight. Then she remembered. She'd tried so hard to be helpful by picking up the plank for Maddox and his brothers that she hadn't even thought about tying off her horse. She would have been left afoot.

Not so tragic here in town. But if she, or her character, ever did that on the trail, Ketchum would become a greater laughingstock than she'd made of him already.

Yes, Gage Newcomb was right and honest to a fault.

Maybe she needed to reevaluate just how much of that she wanted in her depiction of Ketchum…or even in her real-life hero one day.

"Tomorrow at ten, then," she said, neither admitting nor denying that she had made a greenhorn's mistake in not securing the horse's reins earlier. Dealing with horses was something she was supposed to already be good at.

"Make it dawn. Or just before," Gage countered. "Out where the wedding was held."

"The children may have to come with me," she said. She and Snow had not yet discussed the schedule her sister planned in regard to taking turns watching Ollie and Thaddeus. The children might have to tag along for some of the lessons, and Willow wasn't sure she wanted that to happen.

"I'm guessing you won't have to worry about that this time." Gage offered her a hand up into the buggy.

"Oh?" She accepted his help and placed her palm in one of his as his other hand clutched her waist and boosted her up and into the seat.

The sound of retching echoed from just outside the livery.

Ollie stuck her head around the door. "Aunt Willow? Uh… Thad just threw up some brown-and-purple lumpy stuff all over his Sunday shoes. You ought to see it. Must have been some of that… Uh-oh… gotta go."

She disappeared suddenly and her little hand gripped the side of the door. From the sound of it, two unfortunate souls were losing their overabundance of desserts.

Gage extended Willow a hand back down from the buggy and she accepted it.

"You grab a bucket and head to the trough." He pointed to one of the stalls. "I'll find something to wash their faces with."

"Deal," Willow agreed, hoping this was the last time trouble visited her at the livery. Even if she managed to get the children cleaned up and settled down enough to endure the jostling ride home, she was never going to hear the end of it when Snow learned what had made them sick.

As the first edges of twilight stretched purple fingers along the eastern horizon, Gage reined the buggy to a halt in front of Daisy's barn. It had taken half an hour or more to make the fifteen-minute trip from town because he'd had to stop along the way and let the children relieve their sour stomachs over the sides of the buggy. He'd have to clean up the buggy once they were safely in their beds and before he headed back.

Despite his offer to take them to the doctor before leaving town, Willow had insisted they head straight for Daisy's instead. She'd been certain the doctor would only confirm that Ollie and Thad had eaten too much and nothing but a long night's rest would provide the cure.

Gage settled the reins and got out just as she exhaled a long, deep breath. She sat in the backseat, quiet and unmoving now as the pair of rascals pressed against her, one under each shoulder and both sound asleep. The half bucket of water and rags she'd used to mop and soothe their faces still sat between her long legs, dampening her skirt.

"We made it," she whispered. "Before nightfall. Thank you."

"You're welcome." Gage reached for Ollie. "I'll take this one in and come back for the boy in a few minutes. You just sit there and rest. You've got to be tired from trying to keep them clean."

"I'm okay." Her eyes met his for a moment and held. "They needed me. I couldn't do much but offer a rag and some sympathy."

"It helped. I sure couldn't have done any better and was glad you asked me to take the reins." When Gage nestled Ollie against his shoulder, she curled herself into him and snuggled.

He would have never dreamed a feisty handful such as Ollie could feel so delicate and small, her breath brushing against his neck in warm tiny puffs of air. Something inside him softened inexplicably, crumbling a hard edge he'd erected long ago.

"Be right back," he told Willow, surprised by his reaction and not sure why he had given it any thought, much less let it bother him. Holding a sleeping child was a wonder.

Gage took quick strides to the house. At the door, he managed to knock softly so he wouldn't wake Ollie and hoped that the cook or Willow's sister were already aware that the buggy had arrived.

Where were Shepard Hutton and his men? One of them should have already been helping Willow with Thad or, in the least, putting away the team and buggy. Maybe they'd show up before he returned to get Thaddeus.

The door opened and Snow stepped back to let him in. Her eyes focused immediately on Ollie and she rushed up to examine her. "What's wrong? Is she all right? Is she—?"

"Shh," Gage whispered. "Lead me to her room."

Snow stepped back and looked past Gage.

"Don't worry. The boy's okay. They've just got bellyaches. I'll tell you all about it once we've got them to bed. Now, please, point the direction."

Her long white braid of hair flipped against her back as she turned and moved upstairs to lead the way. Gage followed, taking the stairs two at a time. Snow opened a door to the right of the second-story landing and he found a sparsely furnished but comfortable-looking room, where he placed Ollie on the bed.

Her aunt quickly took over. Like a wolf making sure each pack member had returned for the day, Gage waited a second to see this little one was in good care before setting out for the boy.

Snow's palm pressed against both of Ollie's cheeks and felt the little girl's forehead before she moved over to the armoire and pulled out fresh clothing. Glancing up at Gage, she whispered, "Go on. I'll put her in some clean nightclothes. Shut the door behind you and tell my sister to bring Thad up immediately."

Gage obeyed as if she'd given an order, but her tone was soft. Her eyes, on the other hand, spoke volumes of disapproval he suspected would reach Willow before the night ended. He'd have to make certain Snow understood that Willow was innocent of any wrongdoing in the ice-cream incident.

He passed the cook as he headed out the door. "The kids are sick," he explained. "Too much ice cream."

Myrtle wiped her hands on her apron and nodded as she followed him and held the door open for Willow, who approached the porch with Thaddeus in her arms. "This isn't the first bellyache those two have come home with, I assure you. You'd think they'd learn their lesson by now."

"It wasn't their fault. It was mine," Willow apologized. "I shouldn't have let myself get distracted."

Gage took the boy from her arms and headed into

the house ahead of her. "I'll carry him up if one of you will turn down his covers and find him some clean clothes. Snow's doing the same for Ollie."

Willow started to head upstairs but she quickly turned. "Maybe you better go ahead of me, Myrtle. I think I know which room is his, but I have no clue what he'd want to wear or where to find it. I j-just haven't had that much time to get to know him yet. Either of them."

She'd taken all the blame when it had been only a third hers. The hesitancy in her voice regarding knowing her nephew well enough stirred sympathy within Gage. He hardened his feelings most of the time to people's persuasions, accustomed to rough customers who tried to take advantage of his sense of justice. But something about Willow won him over easily and he didn't like being that easy to sway. It felt unnatural. As if his whole system were some kind of river that wanted to change course where she was concerned.

"No problem." Myrtle led them upstairs to Thad's room and quickly pulled out a pair of knickers made of fleece. She pointed for Gage to lay him down on the bed. "He hates to wear a nightshirt of any kind, so his ma sews these for him. Spoiled little brat already, even though he's only been in the family for a short while."

Though her words were harsh, the cook brushed the boy's hair back from his brow, her expression soft with affection.

No sooner than Myrtle started changing Thaddeus's soiled clothing did Snow show up at his door, clearing her throat.

Gage turned the same time as Willow and they collided. She stiffened immediately as he reached out to make sure she didn't fall, but he couldn't tell if her reaction was to him or the fact that her sister stood wagging her forefinger at them to move out into the hallway.

He took note that Willow gently closed the door behind her, leaving Myrtle to finish putting the boy to bed.

Gage could sense Willow tensing as she faced her sister again, her shoulders squaring off, her chin lifting.

"Yes?" she asked.

"Care to tell me why these two are so sick?" Snow's arms folded into each other as her feet braced apart, making her look as though she were a general demanding answers from his soldiers.

"I'll be glad to, but for the sake of not waking them, let's move downstairs."

It surprised Gage that Willow sounded so calm and in control as she swept past her older sister. He didn't have to be an almost blind man to see that Snow intimidated Willow to no end.

He followed both ladies and offered to take care of the buggy.

"No." Snow waved him to a chair in front of the

settee in the parlor. "I'd like to hear your version of what she's about to tell me."

"It'll be the same as hers," he said, looking Snow McMurtry squarely in the eyes and not accepting the seat she offered.

She blinked before he did, showing that she hadn't expected him to defy her or defend Willow so blatantly. Snow, apparently, was a woman accustomed to having her way. Maybe part of Willow's reason for wanting to learn more was so she could operate more confidently alongside her sister. He'd have to help her any way he could with that. As much as Willow would allow him to.

"Would you prefer I stay, Willow, or put the buggy away?" he asked again. "Doesn't look like any of your men are around to put away the team. I don't mind doing it for you."

"They'll be back later. We gave them the rest of the day off," Snow informed him. "I'm surprised you didn't see any of them in town. I would have guessed you had found them at the saloon."

"We didn't go there," Willow said. "Just the diner and the livery. Another place or two."

Gage wondered if she'd deliberately not mentioned the mercantile or just didn't think it was important enough to add to her list of where she'd been. He could have spoken up and told them neither Shepard Hutton nor any of their other hired hands had chosen to spend their time off in the saloon.

They were nowhere in sight when he'd checked to see if the thief was there.

Where did men spend their free time other than a saloon in these parts? Holed up playing poker, maybe? They could have done that without going to town. Paying court to some of the eligible belles or widows in the area? Seemed most of them had been over at the diner frowning at Willow.

He needed to check out this group of wranglers a little closer and see how they chose to acquaint themselves with the rest of the community. Maybe after the lesson with Willow in the morning, he could take a better look around and see what he could find out about the wranglers.

Not that it was any of his business, but Gage's gut instinct said to walk on the safe side and make it his business. Just in case.

He peered out the front door and realized that twilight was throwing a blanket over the sun, setting the horizon afire in a final blaze of golden glory to keep the Texas prairie warm until dawn. "Better get that buggy put away. I'll see you come morning, Willow."

"You can stay the night," she offered. "There's plenty of room in the barn, if you don't want to go back tonight. I'm sure we've got plenty of supper cooked, if you're hungry, and you should be. You didn't eat much this morning at the reception and nothing while we were in town."

"We have the food left over from the wedding. No problem," Snow reminded him.

Gage shook his head and pinched the lapel of his new frock coat. "Gotta get out of these and into my usuals. Not the kind of thing to be wearing if we're going roping in the morning. Everything I own is back in town."

"So you two are roping tomorrow?" Snow studied her sister. "Did you plan on taking the kids with you?"

Willow started to speak up, but Gage interrupted her. "I was hoping maybe you'd let them sleep in awhile, Miss McMurtry. Particularly since they are so sick tonight. We'll be finished by eight or nine at the latest. Then she can resume helping care for the children. That way, I don't upset anybody's schedule."

Snow mulled it for a moment and nodded. "That sounds fair enough, and making those two stay in bed for a few hours longer would give me and Myrtle a chance to get some other things done we need to do around here. You can plan on it, Will."

That was the first time he recalled Snow saying her sister's name with any hint of affection.

Willow certainly didn't look as if she were happy about how she'd been addressed. In fact, her cheeks turned a shade darker than her hair and her eyes shone as if someone had lit a fire in them.

"I didn't know I had to get permission." Willow's voice came calmer than her features appeared. "I already told Gage I would meet him. If you need me to take the children with us, we will."

Snow frowned and held a palm up as if trying to

hold back the argument. "No need to get testy about it. There's no reason we can't swap watching the children every other day so each of us has time for ourself. I was going to suggest that once we had a moment to really sit down and discuss it more. You'll remember that neither of us have had any time to do that yet. May I ask why he's teaching you to rope or whatever it is you're planning?"

Gage wanted the real answer to that question, too.

"I'm trying to fit in and learn Texas ways I don't know of or am unsure about, particularly if I decide to settle here in High Plains. I hired him to show me a few things I thought you or Daisy might not have time to teach me and, frankly, the differences in the way a man versus a woman might handle them. I've forgotten a lot of what Grandfather taught us over the years, and I wanted to really know how much of his life was real or made up. Is that so wrong?"

It seemed there was an emotional reason involved. Gage sensed something deeper had compelled her actions. She was trying to hold on to the idea that her grandfather was nothing less than who she'd made him out to be.

Living up to her hero's imagined perfection might explain her fierce desire to do things better.

"He always had you fooled." Snow finally sat down. "You thought he could do no wrong. Grandfather was a great storyteller, sis. We all loved his tales. But nobody's life is as perfect or adventuresome as he made it out to be. There's no measuring up to that. He lived and spoke his truth the way he saw it. The best he could. Can't you see? That's all any of us can do."

Was Snow right in telling Willow that? Gage wondered if he was guilty of doing the exact same thing. Was he pretending that nothing was amiss by hiding his fading eyesight from others so that he could remain a Ranger for as long as possible?

Was there another way to go about living his own truth even when he could not see it anymore?

Had God, who he thought had forsaken him when Hodge pitched the lye into his face, sent him here to High Plains not only to find the man he tracked but to hear these sensible words tonight?

For the first time in six months, he thought he saw an answer glimmering in the darkness he feared would become his future. Maybe God still walked beside him even when Gage hadn't taken the time to talk to Him.

With tomorrow's dawn, he would try walking out of the shadows of wishful speculation and challenge himself to find another path of worth for himself.

God would help him find the right way; all he had to do was listen.

Chapter Ten

The crow of a rooster jarred Willow awake. She was late!

Throwing back the covers, she glanced out the bedroom window as her bare toes reached for the hardwood floor. Dawn poured through the curtains.

As fast as she could, she grabbed the first thing in the armoire that made any sense to wear for an outing throwing loops. Fastening herself into a brown riding skirt and butternut-colored blouse, she decided there was no time to be choosy this morning. Might as well be comfortable.

One glance in the oval mirror attached to the armoire put her in an even worse panic. Her hair looked as if she had wallowed against her pillow like a dog trying to itch himself free of a flea. She did what she could to straighten out the tangles before brushing the strawberry-colored mass away from her face and gathering it at the back of her head with a saffron-colored ribbon. The only style she could manage was letting her hair hang freely like the undocked tail of a pony.

A quick search yielded her kid leather boots scooted far beneath the four-poster bed. Good thing she was long armed enough to reach them without having to take time to find the broom and sweep them out from under. That was one advantage to inheriting her mother's extraordinary height and slender bone structure.

What else did she need to take with her? Willow surveyed the room and decided she ought to include her journal and a sharpened pencil. No, two pencils, in case one broke. Though her memory was fairly good, she wanted to jot down notes if necessary.

The journal still lay open on the reading table, where she'd left it long past midnight. She'd stayed up writing, making certain she'd reached the page goal she'd immediately set for herself in order to meet Biven's requested deadline for the first story. She'd left Will Ketchum reading signs in Dead Man's Gulch to make sure he found his way to safety. Just as she'd done deciding which way was the right way to town. Maybe something she would learn about roping today would spur a unique solution in how Ketchum ultimately saved himself.

Better get gone or Gage would think she'd changed her mind about meeting him.

Willow grabbed the journal and pencils, then closed the door to her mess of a room. She would clean it up later when she returned. As she tiptoed past the other bedrooms, she wondered if anyone else was already up. No aromas drifted from downstairs hinting that Myrtle had started cooking for the day, and the house remained quiet.

She finally paused at the front door just long enough to consider a quick visit to the kitchen. A piece of fruit or something from the pie safe that had been left over from yesterday sounded the most logical choice to grab, but that would take time she didn't have. Breakfast could wait until after the roping lesson.

Heading out, Willow glanced toward the barn and wished she'd instructed Shepard or one of his men to have a horse saddled for her already, but she'd been busy writing and never got around to connecting with any of them when they returned last night.

She couldn't blame anyone but herself that there wasn't time to saddle up now, so she'd just have to walk the distance to meet Gage. It wasn't that far beyond the main house and surrounding buildings. At least, she didn't remember it to be. Following the stream that led to the lake should take her to the field of verbena quickly enough.

As she passed the barn and salt shed, she saw Shepard letting the horses out of the corral and into the pasture for the morning. She'd thought he and his men might sleep in a bit after their long evening away, but he seemed back on his schedule. A man with a good work ethic.

Maybe she'd take a few lessons from him. But she still hadn't questioned him about why he'd removed his gold tooth. There had simply been no time to talk to him yet. If Snow occupied Ollie and Thad for a short while this morning, as she said she would, then there might prove a few moments for that talk with Shepard later.

Willow waved and he tipped his hat in acknowledgment. So far he'd been the sort of man who, while not being unfriendly, didn't invite her any closer. Maybe that was one of those unwritten Texas codes between hired hand and employer. Or maybe Texas men just took more time than most to show a bent toward friendliness. The Texas women she'd experienced in High Plains could certainly attest to that! Maybe that was why Snow had been acting so sour since she arrived. She'd turned Texan on her.

The walk to the meeting place took longer than Willow expected. The bright light of dawn stretched far and wide, revealing the brilliant blue of the Texas sky and the rolling green grass of the vast prairie. Daisy's guests must have worked up a real hunger yesterday leaving their wagons and buggies back at the barn to walk all this way to the reception tables. It hadn't seemed that far yesterday when she'd headed back with Gage and the children to take the breakfast baskets to Shepard and his men, but then her mind had been occupied with repaying the ladies for her misguided steps concerning the bouquet.

Just ahead, the stream pooled between two gentle

slopes of the prairie, forming the lake where the cold beverages had chilled. Above the slope on the opposite side of the lake, she saw Gage Newcomb's tall dark figure standing near the headstones and wooden crosses that made up the fenced-in family cemetery.

Wearing his hat and burnt-at-the-edges-but-clean duster, he slapped a lariat against his right leg as if he were counting her footsteps. His legs were braced apart, his back to the rising sun. From the slight breeze that drifted her way, she noticed his hobbled horse indulging himself in a patch of some kind of greenery that smelled like mint.

She couldn't see Gage's eyes, nor could she read his expression, but his stance hinted he might have a word or two to say about her being late. She might as well get her apology over with.

Willow hurriedly passed the horse. "Sorry," she said, sweeping beyond Gage to place her journal and pencils on a bench that offered mourners a place to sit and rest. "I overslept."

"You didn't bring a rope? Or a horse?" Disapproval echoed in his voice.

"I figured you would have the rope." She wished now she'd followed her first instinct and ridden here. She probably would have remembered to grab a rope. "I didn't know I'd need a horse. You told me what I did wrong with mine yesterday. I thought we could move on from that."

"So you just want to know how to rope from a ground position. Not while riding?"

He surprised her with that question. She supposed there was a difference in how it was done in motion. But not wanting to admit she hadn't even considered both ways, Willow simply said, "I'll see how well I do standing still. Then we'll figure out whether or not I need to know more."

She definitely needed to be more specific in the future about what and how much she wanted him to teach her about a subject.

He quit tapping the lariat against his thigh. "Your choice."

Willow glanced around and wondered why he chose this particular location. "I don't see a stump to practice on."

"You won't find one around here. Well, maybe a lightning-struck one," he amended. "Trees are precious commodity in the Panhandle. We either grow 'em full crowned for shade or to act as wind barriers. If they're not good any longer, we pull 'em up by the root and burn 'em for fuel. You're gonna have to rope other things today, like maybe one of these headstones or the bench. Thought I'd try you out with this stone marker. Or maybe a fence picket will do."

Willow hesitated. The thought of roping a headstone had never entered her mind. Given her talent for knocking things over, what if she pulled the rope too taut and yanked the stone out of place? That would cause her nightmares for weeks. "I'm game for a picket. Let me try that first."

"All right, show me what you know." He offered her the lariat.

"You're supposed to show me, remember? You're the teacher. I'm the student." She didn't grab the rope and instead waited for him to start the lesson.

"So I take it your grandfather never showed you how to do this?"

"I watched Grandfather plenty of times, but seeing how it's done and doing it are separate matters altogether."

Gage faced the fence and began slipping the rope through the small loop he made at the end of the lariat. "This little end is called a honda. Form a noose about a foot or two wide."

She admired the dexterity of Gage's long fingers as they worked.

"You're right-handed," he said.

The fact that he'd noticed that about her pleased Willow. But why shouldn't he notice? A good teacher should become aware of his student's preferences.

"If you were left-handed, you would do this directly opposite what I'm gonna show you now," he said. "Hold the loop lightly in your right hand a foot or so from the honda and coil the rest of the lariat in your left hand. Leave enough rope between the noose and the coil so it doesn't kink. Say about five or six feet."

Willow watched, wishing she had her journal in her hands right about now. She would have been writing madly to get this all down. But she didn't want to stop him to go pick it up.

Gage nodded toward the fence. "Plant yourself in front of the target. Relax your wrist, then slowly swing the rope over your head, right to left. It should look like a rawhide wagon wheel revolving horizontally over your head."

He had a way with description she could use in her story.

Her breathing sped up to keep time with the *whoosh, whoosh, whoosh* of the rope cutting the air.

"Now you've got to swing your arm forward and bring your wrist down to shoulder level, then extend your arm. After you've done that, you'll open your palm and cast the loop toward your target. Let me show you."

The power of his arm and wrist kept a steady rhythm as the rope revolved and extended toward the fence picket. Willow was amazed at how he didn't miss a beat with his wrist as he talked. So calm. So collected. So persistent.

"The force you used to thrust the loop forward determines how far the lariat goes." His words of instruction matched rhythm with each flick of his wrist. "Don't worry if you don't rope it the first time. Practice helps you learn how to reach your target or not overthrow."

"I doubt I'll ever overthrow," she confessed, imagining what kind of strength it must take just to be accurate, much less too powerful.

She watched him blink, then squint hard seconds before his wrist and arm suddenly stopped revolving. The rope landed and Gage pulled the length of the lariat coiled in his left hand, tightening the loop around the picket. Perfect!

"You ready to give it a try?" He walked over and unfastened the loop, then recoiled the rope to its original position.

Willow shook her head and finally grabbed her writing instruments, taking a seat on the bench. "I want to write it all down so I can remember it later."

She opened her journal and began recording the images so vivid in her mind.

"Like I said, practice is the way to make yourself good at it." He turned around and built his loop again, then threw it a second time, only to miss.

She looked up from her scribbling. "Why did you miss?"

"The truth?"

"Always." She stared and wondered why he'd even considered being anything but honest with her.

"You distracted me."

She usually messed herself up and didn't mind taking the blame if she was truly guilty of causing trouble for someone else, but she'd been nowhere near his target. "How did I do that?"

Gage retrieved his rope and strolled over to sit beside her on the bench.

"I let you. I was paying more attention to your hair than I was the picket."

"My hair?" Her hand dropped the pencil and immediately shot up to feel the top of her head. Had her ribbon shifted? The tail drooped? Was there still a nest of curls she hadn't managed to untangle with the brush?

Embarrassment heated Willow's cheeks. "I had to hurry with it since I was late getting here. I usually brush it better than this."

Gage reached and stopped her from patting her head to check for disarray. When her arm slowly returned to her side, he ran his fingers through the cascade of curls hanging down her back.

"Settle down," he said softly. "You've done nothing wrong. I've just never seen the sun shine so strong in a woman's hair. I thought I was only imagining the streaks that look like copper running through it. Then I found myself wondering if it would be as warm and welcoming to the touch as it looked." He leaned a little closer, his breath brushing her temple as he whispered, "It is."

A shiver of attraction ran through Willow while he explored the texture of a curl between his fingers.

She didn't know whether to be flattered or insulted that he felt at liberty to be *this* honest. If this was what he'd meant earlier at the livery in asking for payment after each lesson, she would certainly have a say about it. As soon as she could find the good sense to speak again.

"Come on. Set down the book or journal or whatever that is," he said. "Let's see how well you build a loop."

Gage rose, ending her quandary about his being so near. She laid the journal down and accepted the lariat he insisted she take.

"Which picket do you choose?" He took up a place directly behind her.

She pointed. "The one just above the gate latch."

"Show me what you thought you saw me do."

Though he stood far enough back to give her room to navigate the rope, Willow sensed the power of his eyes focusing on her every movement, studying, weighing, judging her ability to find accuracy.

She hesitated. It had looked so easy. Taking a deep breath, she did her best to remember each step. Her arm was getting tired twisting that wagon wheel over and over above her.

"Trust yourself." His words jolted her as she cast the loop to reach her target.

It landed dead center.

"Did you see that?" she exclaimed. "I did it the first time!"

"You're gonna be good at it. Now try it again."

His compliment thrilled Willow and gave her courage to try again. Several more attempts met with the same effect and her arm felt as if it was loosening up more.

"You've got good eyes and quick timing with your wrist. That's half the battle. Keep after it until you've lassoed a dozen pickets or more." Gage pointed to the bench. "Try something bigger now, keeping in mind how large to build the noose."

Willow did as he instructed but missed when she made the attempt, the force of the rope slinging her journal and pencils off the bench.

She hurried to try again, only to stop short an inch away from grabbing the rope. There, crawling across her journal and too close to the noose she'd thrown, was a spiky creature with a round body and blunt nose. Horns extended from its gray-and-yellow-tinted head. She shrieked and moved backward.

Gage came to her rescue, picking up the lizard-like reptile and opening his palm to show it now lying on its back, completely limp and playing dead. "It won't hurt you. Just a little old horned lizard. Probably unburied itself from the sand to sun itself or head over to one of those ant hills for some breakfast."

She shuddered and grabbed the rope, her journal and pencils while she could. "I say how about we help it on its way?"

Gage chuckled and set the creature down. The lizard darted away. "You know she could teach you a thing or two about hitting your target."

"She?" Willow wondered how he'd made that determination so quickly.

"She's about four and a half inches long. The males are usually two and a half to three." Gage took the rope from Willow and started recoiling it.

"Probably making her way over to bring breakfast back to her babies."

Curiosity urged Willow to ask, "How could she teach me anything?"

"Though she wouldn't have bitten you, if she felt threatened at all, she might have squirted a stream of blood from the corner of her eye, deliberately aiming it at you. I've seen one hit a coyote four or five feet away."

His nose wrinkled. "The blood is foul smelling and must sting something fierce, as loud as that coyote howled. I'd say it's a pretty effective defense to scare someone or something off. I've never seen one miss when it's fighting for its life. A little sure shot, you might say. Aim and mean where you throw it. That's what she could teach you."

Gage motioned toward his horse as he took the rope from her. "That's enough roping for now. What do you say we head on in and see what we can get into back at the barn? Maybe show you how to replace a shoe if your horse ever throws one when you're afield. That's knowledge that'll serve you well anytime."

"I could use something to eat soon," she admitted. "Didn't have time to have breakfast before I came." Willow saw an opportunity to learn more about Gage than he'd revealed. Falling in step beside him, she remembered the spider at the livery, the lizard and now his mention of the horseshoe. "You seem to have a good knowledge of God's beasts. Are you a horse doctor or something?"

"Never stayed anywhere long enough to do that." When they reached his mount, he undid the hobble and offered her a hand up.

She shook her head. That wouldn't be fair to him. "I'll walk."

Gage chose to do the same and took the horse's reins, leading it toward the lake and the stream that would guide them back to the main house. His stride matched Willow's as they ambled at a steady pace.

"Lived most of my life outdoors," he finally continued. "It's inevitable to learn a few things about those of us who share the wide-open spaces."

"Surely you don't just roam around and live life hand to mouth like the mountain men used to do, do you?" As a person who had a goal to achieve and a desire for a measure of success, Willow couldn't imagine finding happiness living life purely by the moment and, more important, all alone. "Don't you like company?"

He took a long time to answer. "Hard to miss it when you've never had much."

That confession revealed more than if he'd gone on with endless conversation. As they followed the stream, he said no more and she wondered what he was thinking.

He seemed perfectly content with his own thoughts, where she, on the other hand, decided to continue rattling on at the mouth about how she liked being with people even when it took a little while for the appre-ciation to become mutual.

Her mind ran amok with a handful of questions she would have gladly asked if he'd been in a more talkative mood.

Did he prefer being such a loner? Was he the kind of man her grandfather had told her about who sup-posedly found joy in riding the long trail? Did he ride alone or prefer to work in a company of men? Grandfather's tales of the first Rangers said the job required men willing to give up all to protect and serve others. Like an apostle of sorts. Was Gage that type of man?

The desire to ask him if he was or had ever been a Ranger kept building every time she was near Gage. That she couldn't let it go bothered her, but she knew the day she would outright ask him wasn't long in coming. She'd never been able to keep her curiosity in rein or her mouth shut for that long!

Willow stole a glance at him, thinking he sure fit the bill of what she thought a Ranger might be. Tall, rugged, strong…and not very talkative, she had to admit grudgingly. Cowboy code insisted that if you're hurting, hide it, according to Grandfather.

What concerned her most was, even if Gage was a Ranger, why would he want to hide that fact from her? It wasn't as if she would tell anyone else but her boss. Biven would be pleased she'd gotten such a reliable source to confirm the facts she used in her story for the paper.

She could even see the possibility of having to tell Snow about his profession if he stayed around the place for much longer. Her sister would want to know he was a lawful man they could trust.

Having a possible Ranger teach her was wise, wasn't it? That was the real issue here.

The longer Willow mulled the question, the more Gage's keeping his counsel bothered her. "Ollie and Thad finally settled in close to midnight," she blurted, hoping that mentioning the children would spur his gift of gab. "They won't be wanting any ice cream for a while."

"Glad they're better."

She waited for him to say something more. He didn't. Well, that had gone over about as well as the preacher passing the collection plate an extra time around.

Willow felt increasingly uncomfortable as her thoughts returned to all she'd been considering. Might it ultimately prove a big mistake to count on Gage in the event he was actually a member of Ketchum's profession? Was she setting herself up for failure and hadn't even realized it?

A man who was Ranger smart would figure out the reason behind her actions soon enough. Would he walk away thinking she'd used him? Or mocked him?

She didn't think of Gage in that way. He was simply research. She truly admired and respected what she knew of him so far. The only real aggravation she had with him was his bent toward keeping his thoughts to himself. *Speak up, man!* she screamed silently in her impatience.

"What would you like to concentrate on next?" he suddenly asked. "Shooting, shoeing or campfire cooking?"

He'd spoken. "Campfire cooking on the next day I don't have the children to watch," she said. "Maybe show me how to braid a rope on a day they're with me."

"Whatever you say."

He'd had her there a second, cast her a line and hooked her, then threw her back into the deepness of her thoughts. He closed himself off as quickly as he had offered an opening. It showed he had little practice in being good company.

She'd considered him friendly enough up until now. He didn't try to boss her around anywhere near as much as Snow had. And even when he'd made her temper flare, they'd both gotten over it pretty quickly. No one got along perfectly, did they? Especially if one of them wasn't the sort to want to talk things out. It pestered Willow to no end that he was perfectly fine with holding his tongue.

As her character did sometimes. Sat there in her mind's eye looking as though a gag had been stuffed in his mouth, refusing to give her a clue as to how she could discover his story or anything about him.

Was that what Gage was doing? Gagging himself so he wouldn't reveal any more of his past?

Stubborn pride wouldn't let her leave it alone and

just enjoy the walk home. She aimed to find out more about him, but she didn't want to anger Gage. He might eventually discover how she'd messed up her fictional Ranger's worth. In fact, she expected him to live up to a Ranger's creed and would be disappointed in him if he proved anything less.

But would he put her chance to make things right with Biven in jeopardy? Should she tread a little more cautiously where *his* pride might be concerned?

They'd known each other less than three full days but she had already come to a point of looking forward to spending time with Gage. Learning what he had to teach. Discovering that she liked to impress him. Somehow it had come to matter what he thought of her attempts. And what he would think of how she would present his choice of lifestyle to the readers.

A sense of regret filled Willow, saddening her. What if once he found out why she was trying so hard to prove herself, he decided never to see her again?

"Will you be available tomorrow?" She hoped that she wouldn't have to skip any days, whether or not she had to care for the children. "I'll be in town."

"If you need me."

"Where do you want to meet?" she asked. "Choose somewhere we can just sit and braid rope…and chew the fat."

"In front of the barbershop next to the bathhouse, there's a couple of whittling benches that don't usually get crowded until after the morning stage rolls in," he informed her. "How does ten o'clock sound? We can sit and watch people come and go."

"Sounds fine to me. I'll look forward to it. And don't worry, I'll pick up what I need at the mercantile before I meet you. You don't have to bring a thing."

Sometime during the past three days, Gage Newcomb had become her friend. Someone she would want as part of the tribe she so longed to be involved with.

If she had to give up his companionship, it wouldn't be a loss she'd take lightly.

No longer paying attention to her path, Willow nearly stumbled on uneven ground, her right kid boot bending at the ankle, only to correct itself with a wrenching pop. She clutched her journal to her breast so she wouldn't lose it and gritted her teeth against the instant pain.

He abruptly dropped the horse's reins and grabbed her, pulling her closer to offer support. She ended up with her arm wrapped around his waist and her nose buried in his duster. He might have washed the trail coat, but the smell of smoke still lingered in its threads. Maybe she could give it a good scrubbing for him for catching her and not letting her fall on her face just now.

"You hurt?"

She shook her head and leaned back, testing her sore ankle by putting weight on her foot again. Nothing broken, not even sprained. It was just going to ache like nobody's business for the rest of the day.

As clumsy as she was, she would have never made

it past toddler stage if she hadn't had strong bones. Willow tried to laugh off her embarrassment. "Just my usual lack of gracefulness. Thanks, Gage. Guess one never knows when you're going to need a little help. Having company pays off sometimes."

Gage didn't let her step away, instead taking her hand and lacing his fingers through hers. She was trying to act as if she needed no help, but he had to make certain she could walk easily on her own before they went much farther.

He quickly retrieved the reins and waited on Willow. Inhaling the lingering scent of sunshine and wildflowers that permeated the air about her, he realized he would never recall this particular fragrance again without thinking of it as the one that belonged to a morning spent in her company. Yes, sometimes company had its value.

"What will you do with the rest of today?" he asked, watching her limp with each new step. "I think we ought to save the horseshoeing for later down the road."

"I'm perfectly fine," she insisted, unthreading her fingers from his and trying to increase her pace, "and I don't want to waste my free time."

"Don't be startled," he warned, taking quick strides to lift Willow and cradle her in his arms. "You're going to ride the rest of the way."

She squirmed for only a second as he settled her into the saddle and insisted she take the reins.

"There, that better?"

Willow glared at him a moment, then finally nodded. "Okay, I admit it. It hurts and I'm hardheaded. You win. Now, where am I going to put this?"

She twisted around to reach his saddlebags but couldn't.

Gage took the journal and slipped it inside his buttoned-up shirt against his belly. "There, easily solved. Where are your pencils?"

She shrugged. "I lost them somewhere between shrieking at the lizard and falling over my own two feet. I can never keep track of everything, it seems."

He rattled off a poem.

There was an old Texan, roamed his country far and wide
Found the light of his freedom in the quiet, starlit sky
No slave to a whistle, no prisoner to a street
He was partner to the wind and the horse between his knees
Needed little to earn a living but hardened muscle, savage grit
Wanted ownership of nothing but a blessing to never quit

"That was beautiful," she complimented. "Nice way to put my priorities in their proper place. So what if I lost a pencil? Who wrote it?"

Gage stared into the distance, remembering the

day he'd buried his father. He was glad the images would at least fade from his sight someday, whether or not they ever did in his mind. "A boy who once lost everything that ever mattered to him."

"You wrote that, didn't you?" Sympathy softened her voice.

"I suppose many of us try our hand at writing a time or two in our lives." He'd never shared the poem with anyone before and was surprised he offered the words so easily now.

He had purposefully corralled his bent for poetry and writing stories behind the youth he'd been forced to let go of long before he became a man. Now that he was losing sight, what use would it do to loosen that rein again?

The poem had just come to mind when she spoke of losing something as simple as a pencil.

"I'm guessing you've written more than a time or two if you wrote something like that. You have talent, Gage. Real talent. You ought to pursue that. There's got to be somebody who's interested in buying it for publication. It made me feel something here." She pressed her palm over her chest. "Only real writers can do that."

Gage wished he hadn't opened up this vein her thoughts were taking. She could be persistent when she chose to set her mind to something. "If I write at all, it's only for myself."

"Well, I can't imagine being good enough to sell

my writing but not wanting to do anything with it," she blurted. "That's a waste of God-given talent."

She sounded angry with him. He'd suspected she nurtured an interest in writing when she'd preferred to jot things down instead of actually doing them earlier when he'd shown her how to rope. "Is that the real reason you're trying to learn these new skills? Plan on writing about them?"

Her eyes widened as if she'd let a cougar out of its cage. The fact that she wanted to be paid for her writing meant nothing to him. To each his own. But the look she gave him affected him immensely, reminding Gage of the beautiful palomino color of her eyes. He would remember this day for several reasons, but her eyes would occupy his thoughts for nights to come and long after the time his own saw no more.

"T-take a look at my journal and you'll see. I write poetry, too," she finally confessed. "Only nowhere near as polished as yours."

He felt the journal where it balanced between his shirt and stomach. "These are your personal thoughts. You don't have to show me."

"No, really. I want you to tell me what you think." She seemed over whatever hesitation held her back before and pointed her finger at his belly. "Get it out and thumb it open anywhere. You'll see."

Willow wouldn't let him decline. She rested her arms on the saddle horn until Gage finally gave in and lifted the journal from his shirt. "Any page?"

"Start at the first," she said, "but it got much better the more I wrote."

He opened the cover and read a few pages. She really meant what she said. She liked to write. It showed in the variety of her notes, in how hard she tried to let the words paint an image or evoke a feeling inside the reader. Page after page was filled with poems and descriptions of scenery, words she must have heard people say to each other, different phrasings and notations about accents, a collection of traits she found interesting enough to reveal about a character's particular personality.

Gage thumbed farther, finding notes about reading signs and tracking. A brief story she must have written recently revealed she was trying her hand at fiction.

His admiration for her grew. If she meant to apply the lessons she learned from him, she was smart enough to realize that truth in her work would make her fictional world more believable. Though she had a long way to go in spit-polishing her material, she had the curiosity needed to pursue the craft.

When he thought he'd read enough to satisfy her, he glanced up and saw she was looking at him in anticipation.

"Well?" Hope filled her tone.

He didn't want to discourage her by saying she could still use some work on it. That these were good first attempts. She was looking for encouragement. "Like I said before, success comes with trying. Now you need to practice, practice, practice, and that means you'll have to be persistent in filling these pages and others like them."

She looked crestfallen. "You mean I've got a long way to go, don't you? Weeks, maybe?"

"You in some kind of hurry?" he asked, closing the journal and preparing to slip it down his shirt again. "I'm just saying I think a true writer takes whatever time he or she needs to get a poem or story or book right. If you want to be a storyteller, take the time to get it right."

"Don't put it there again," she insisted, leaning back stiffly in the saddle. "I can do the same myself."

He handed her the journal and she stuffed it in the squared-off collar of her butternut blouse. "See? Perfectly safe. My foot is throbbing quite a bit now. I think we best be on our way."

Something else was bothering Willow, and he hoped he hadn't insulted her. He hadn't meant to. She'd asked him his opinion and he'd told her as gently as he could that she needed more work. Now it was up to her to either reject what he said or take that suggestion and let it help her.

Pouting was not a skill that would get any writer very far.

Nor any blind man, even if it meant she no longer cared to share his company.

Chapter Eleven

The next morning started off much better than the last. Willow woke ready to face the challenge of whatever the day brought. She had nursed her sore ankle after Gage returned to town yesterday and used the rest of her free time to write and get further along with her story.

Ketchum had ended up hurting his foot. She'd giggled as she wrote him tumbling over a rock that had suddenly sprouted legs and transformed into an armadillo that had camouflaged itself to bask in the sun. The story ended with Ketchum roping things he needed so he didn't have to walk. A tangle between a coyote and a horned lizard kept him entertained while he ate and rested his foot.

Her boss and readers would surely love the realism depicted in this part of the tale.

When Ollie and Thad learned she was headed to town to restock her supply of paper, they had begged to come along. Both stood beside her now, waiting patiently as she paid for her purchases at the mercantile.

She fished into her skirt pocket for money. "Would you like some candy for later? Licorice or salt taffy?"

"No, thank you," they replied in unison.

Both still hadn't quite gotten over the ice-cream incident. Neither had mentioned visiting the diner even once on the ride to town.

"Just one more item, Mr. Pickens—" Willow turned back to the merchant "—and that will be all. I'd like a copy of Walt Whitman's *Leaves of Grass*, please."

Ollie grumbled as he climbed a small ladder behind the counter and retrieved the book from a top shelf lined with volumes. "You ain't gonna read us no poetry today, are ya?" she complained.

Willow groaned inwardly hearing her niece's misuse of their beloved language. "No, the book is a gift for someone."

The child exhaled a sigh of relief. "Good. My stomach is still queasy. Listening to that would have made it worse."

The merchant placed the book inside the woven bag she'd brought with her to carry her purchases and rang up the total. "You want to pay now or would you prefer I set up an account for you, Miss McMurtry?"

She hadn't had time to visit the bank yet, but neither did she plan on staying in High Plains longer than the two months she'd promised. If she stayed any longer than that, she would transfer her monthly stipend here. "I'll just pay as I go for now. Maybe I'll change my mind later."

She dug into her pocket and gave him the amount shown on the register.

"Thank you. Oh, and I forgot to tell you." Junior Pickens handed her the bag. "A few of the ladies said if I saw you to be sure and thank you for the handkerchiefs and for buying their lunch yesterday."

Disappointment filled Willow. He'd promised to be discreet. "I thought that was supposed to stay between us."

His Adam's apple sunk low in his thin throat, then rose slowly to find its perch again. "Seems my intended, Hannabelle, was your waitress and she told me about you buying the ladies' meals. Of course, I didn't think nothing of sharing your kindness in sending them the pretty hankies. After all, couples share secrets, don't they?"

His eyes rolled up into his lids. "Well, turns out she heard the ones who picked up their mail talking about the mysterious gifts they'd received. At suppertime last night, she couldn't resist telling her personal friend exactly who had bought the meals and the hankies. That friend told another and then the gossip whipped around so fast that this morning seems like the whole town got wind of your good deeds."

Apology filled his features. "Hannabelle and I haven't been promised to each other long, Miss

McMurtry. I had a hard time telling her she should've kept your secret. Now she's thinks I've called her a gossip and won't speak to me. I'm sure sorry. Guess I should've done what you asked and told *nobody*."

"It's all right, Mr. Pickens. I understand," she said, accepting his apology and whispering a little prayer of blessings for the poor man. He looked embarrassed by his indiscretion. "They would have probably eventually found out anyway. And please feel free to call me Willow. I do wish you and Hannabelle every happiness."

"I'll carry that for you, Aunt Willow." Thad reached up to take the bag from her.

Ollie's fists balled at her tiny hips. "Well, if I was you, I'd march over to that diner and tell that ol' waitress you want that tip back you gave her."

"Time to go. We don't want to be late meeting Mr. Newcomb, do we?" Willow thanked the merchant and rushed the children out of the establishment. Ollie had been daring enough to say what she herself had thought for a second before deciding to be more forgiving.

Once they were settled into the buggy, Willow headed around the corner to find the barbershop and bathhouse. Passing the doctor's and undertaker's offices, she spotted Gage's long, lank form already sitting on a bench in front of the bathhouse waiting on her. He stood a moment and pointed toward a rail on the side of the barbershop where he'd tied his horse.

He must mean for her to corral the team between

the two buildings. As she closed the distance and maneuvered the horses alongside his, Gage arrived to lend a hand.

"I see you brought some friends with you," he said, helping her out of the buggy.

"We didn't even have to ask her if we could come. She just let us." Thaddeus offered the bag to Gage while he climbed down.

Gage took it and turned to help Ollie, but the tomboy had already touched ground. "You both look like you're feeling much better than when I saw you last."

Willow finished making sure the buggy would go nowhere, leaving the horses tied to the rail. When she turned around, she discovered Gage stood there watching to see if she remembered to secure her ride home.

He nodded approval.

She was glad she'd pleased him.

"Do you have breakfast behind you?" he asked. "If you haven't, we could—"

"We ate early," Willow assured him as she fetched a small bundle from the backseat of the buggy. She'd almost forgotten to take her writing utensils with her. Throwing the knitted bundle over one shoulder, she laced her fingers through the two strings that kept it pulled tight. "We preferred to spend our time doing what we came for, so we made sure we ate already."

"We ain't had no ice cream or anything today." Ollie rubbed her stomach. "Don't want none neither."

Willow watched amusement dance in Gage's eyes,

but he was wise enough not to smile at the child. If he had, knowing Ollie, her niece probably would have kicked him.

"What's all this?" Gage peered into the bag of goods as they headed for the benches around the corner.

"I told you I'd bring what we needed to braid with. I hope I thought of everything."

Gage lifted out the book. "Whitman's poems?"

"It's a gift. I thought you'd like it. You haven't let me pay you yet, remember?"

"Thank you. I think he's one of the greats."

It disappointed her when Gage simply put the book back where he'd found it. Maybe he was a man unaccustomed to anyone giving him a gift.

"This ought to do here." Gage halted and set the bag down next to a burlap sack stored beneath the bench where she'd spotted him earlier.

"Is that yours?" Willow wondered if he'd forgotten she said she would bring whatever was necessary.

He nodded. "Thought I'd add a few things I hadn't mentioned or maybe you wouldn't think of. We'll see what you brought first."

She and Gage sat down side by side as the two children stood in front of them. She slipped her knitted pouch off her shoulder and gently nestled it next to her sore ankle.

"If you want your own bench, you'll need to grab a place now or you won't get one later," Gage told the children. "Some of the older men in town like to whittle there or here where the sun's brightest. A good place to see what you're making when you've got old eyes."

Willow glanced at Gage's face. Had he chosen this place for that reason? Were his eyes troubling him?

An ugly possibility reared its head. She'd noticed him squinting on more than one occasion. Blinking rapidly, then squinting, as a matter of fact. The red welts shone even fiercer in the bright glare of sunlight on his face. Had whatever happened to him damaged his eyes, as well?

She would study him closer today and see if what she suspected was true.

"Can we help?" asked Thad, continuing to stand in front of the adults. "I don't want to just sit and watch. When I get bored, things just tend to happen."

"Your choice." Willow bent to take the poetry book out of the sack and set it aside on the bench between her and Gage. Then she grabbed the three strands of yarn Gage had suggested she purchase and handed them to him.

"Good. Looks like you remembered to make them twice the length you needed." Gage started to tie off an end of each piece of yarn with an overhand knot. "What I'm going to show you is a couple of ways to make a rope from scratch. That way if you ever need one in a hurry and don't have one, you can make one yourself."

He showed each of them the knots he'd made.

"This knot is your bowline. Make sure it's just big enough to work a pencil through."

Two pair of little hands reached in and pulled out pencils from the sack to try it themselves. Even Ollie wanted to participate. Willow and the children lined up close together.

"If you were out on the trail somewhere, you could use a small stick or twig instead of the pencil. Now take your pencil or stick and work it through one of the knots." Gage waited for all three to complete the task.

"What if I was by myself and didn't have you to hold the end?" Ollie asked the very question that entered Willow's mind. Gage was the one making it all work.

"Fasten the pencil end to something that will keep it secure, like maybe a saddle horn or around a small but heavy rock. Something stationary." He glanced at the children. "Meaning it won't move. Keep in mind that fastening it to something will take up some of the length you're trying to give yourself. Everybody understand so far?"

All three nodded.

"Now look at your yarn closely. The threads are twisting one direction. That's the direction you need to twist when I tell you to. If it's twisting the same direction as a clock moves, that means a right-handed person created it. If it goes the opposite way, it was made by someone left-handed."

"Hey, this one's a left kind," Thaddeus announced. "Ollie, what do you have?"

"Mine goes like a clock," she grumbled.

"Mine's right twisted," Willow chimed in. "Ollie, would you be more comfortable with Thaddeus's?"

Her niece didn't answer. She just grabbed his and said, "That's better."

Thaddeus shifted places so the two strands wouldn't be crossed over Willow's.

"Okay, you all set?" Gage waited until she and the children each had a firm hold. "Now you're going to twist the end of the yarn that isn't connected to the pencil. Be sure and keep doing that in the same direction it was made."

He touched her hand. "Exactly that way, Willow."

Pleased by his approval, she couldn't help but smile. He smiled back and the skin crinkled at the corners of his eyes. When she dared to meet his gaze, she lost her concentration.

"Hey." Thad's voice rose with satisfaction. "It's getting tighter, making little baby curly things."

"That's what it's supposed to do," Gage assured him. "It will look like coils. Hold the tension tight and don't let your coils kink anywhere."

Amazed at how easy this was, Willow felt as excited as the children to be learning so much. She'd never really looked that closely before at ropes. Maybe that was what Biven had wanted her to do with all her research. Dig a little deeper. Look a little closer.

"I can't wait to write this down," she said, eager to take a few minutes to jot down notes. "I hope I can remember it all."

"You brought your journal?" Gage craned to see the bundle near her ankle.

"She don't go nowhere without it," Ollie said. "Like I did when I was making my daddy list. It's good to write stuff down. I got me a new daddy 'cause I did."

"Well, let's finish up with *making* the rope before you write about it," Gage insisted. "When you're sure you're done twisting your own end, all three of you bring your loose ends together without losing the tension. One of you take that combined strand and twist it in the opposite direction, holding the tension on the whole thing. Make sure it flattens out evenly and doesn't kink. If it hasn't, then you can knot the final end together."

The children let Willow complete the task.

Gage ran his hand up and down the length of it, feeling for kinks. "That gives you a three-strand rope. You could, of course, have plaited those three twisted strands like you would a woman's braid, then tie it off, but this way gives the rope greater strength. Just depends on what you need to use it for."

Gage examined the makeshift rope closely. "And just so you know, if you had to do this by yourself, you could stick your finger right in the middle of your strand after you've got it good and tight, then bring the end up to the bowline knot, twisting it all the way. You would secure the two ends together with another overhand knot and that wouldn't let the doubled strand unravel."

"Whew! That's a lot to remember, like Aunt Willow said," Ollie complained. "You sound like my teacher's big ol' book."

"Want to practice awhile?" Gage caught Willow's attention as the children began talking about school starting soon. "Might make you feel more comfortable with understanding what you're wanting to write about it."

Willow thought she could follow his instructions well enough, but to get a really solid image fixed in her mind, she would definitely have to practice more. "I'll need to go back to the store to get more yarn. I didn't think about all of us having so much fun working with it. Or should we just undo this one and remake it?"

Gage shook his head and reached down to pull out the burlap bundle beneath his feet. "I brought something else for you to practice with."

He reached inside to pull out a long strand of something that looked as if it was part flower, part milkweed and part vine.

"What's that?" Willow asked.

"Old-man's beard." Gage handed her one end of the vine, took out a knife from somewhere inside the back of his boot and began shaving off the feather-like flowers that must have earned the plant its name.

"It's a vine that grows around here," he said.

"Usually by a riverbed, or if you happen to come across some hackberry or cottonwood trees, you might see it climbing up the trunks. It's a creeper. The wind blows the seeds everywhere. Good thing about it is that it's plentiful and grows most of the year. You'll always be able to find some."

Gage kept shaving away the white beards. "I thought I'd show you how to use something natural for a rope if you ever found yourself in need of one out on the trail."

She was glad he hadn't said, *If you ever found yourself in trouble.* That would more likely be the possibility.

"Whatever kind of vine you choose, pick one the hummingbirds flock to. Wasps and hornets stay away from those, so you'd be less likely to get stung."

"Can I help cut?" Thaddeus asked, reaching into his trouser pocket.

Willow remembered the boy's knife. "Not with the shaving, Thad. We'll have to let Gage remove the flowers."

Disappointment furrowed the boy's forehead. His hand returned to his side empty.

"They're actually seed heads." Gage quickly stripped the white beards and left only the pale brown bark. "They can leave a blister if you don't know how to cut them at a proper angle. See how I'm doing it?"

Gage offered each of them a shaved strand. "I'll strip some more while you work on those together.

After that, I want you all to make a rope by yourself once so you'll know how."

Willow went to work with Ollie and Thad. It had seemed so easy a minute ago, but the vine strands had no natural coil to them. How were they supposed to tighten them?

"Reckon we ought to just braid these together?" Ollie reasoned aloud, her tone matching the frustration Willow felt. "Mine ain't twisted any which way."

"Smart thinking," Gage complimented as he finished running the knife down the last yard of vine. "I wondered how well you'd listened."

I was that close to suggesting the same thing, Willow told herself, but she hadn't spoken up fast enough. When she looked up, she saw Gage's eyes twinkling with amusement. He'd guessed she was upset with herself for not being the one to say it first.

A couple of old men ambled over to the bench next to theirs and took a seat, distracting Willow for a moment.

"Good day for whittling. Not a cloud in the sky," said the one with red suspenders as he stared up at the sun overhead, then back at the four of them. "I like wood shaving myself. Never tried vine before."

The other newcomer took out a knife and a small piece of wood from his pocket and began slowly carving it, not saying a word to any of them.

Red Suspenders was obviously a chatterer like her. He made a point of asking all of them about what they were doing. Gage was the only one who didn't reply. The other man beside Red shared Gage's penchant for not talking, it seemed, and focused on his handiwork alone.

Odd how opposites tended to flock together, Willow thought as she went back to work. How long had the two elderly men been friends? she wondered. Dare she ask? Red just might spend the rest of the afternoon giving her an answer.

Though the old man was curious about the steps she and the children took, he was gentleman enough not to criticize or interrupt, as she'd thought he might.

"Done." Willow handed Gage the now braided vine.

When Gage accepted it, their fingers touched once more. Willow's heart raced and she wondered if the children had noticed, but their heads were already bowed and their fingers busy with making a rope all alone.

Her and Gage's eyes met and lingered for a split second before she remembered that Red was the one who'd probably seen what had transpired.

Her attention shifted to the curious old man.

He gave them a quick wink and grinned. "Don't mind me, folks. It takes a few minutes or more for these old bones to ease a groove on a bench before I can settle in enough to start my whittling. Rheumatism, you know. I'll leave you to your business sure enough and mind my own."

"No trouble, pilgrim," Gage finally said. "Wasn't

ignoring you. I just tend to concentrate too hard and turn off voices."

Willow could certainly attest to that, but she didn't think the old codger was referring to Gage's lack of speech right now. Her cheeks tightened with the heat of a blush.

"Nothing personal meant whatsoever." Gage suddenly became more long-winded than he'd been since Willow had met him. "Comes from spending a lot of time on my own."

The quiet man sitting next to Red stopped carving and announced, "I'm cut from the same cloth, partner."

Gage surprised Willow by sharing a chuckle with his kinsman in solitude.

Morning passed quickly into early afternoon as Gage watched Willow and the children discover their skill at braiding a rope. She hadn't said much since he'd wanted to make sure he didn't offend the old whittler by keeping silent. Had he insulted her instead when he'd laughed with the old man's partner?

He hadn't meant to, but Willow sure liked to talk. Gage even found himself wondering if he could endure a full twenty-four hours in her chatty company. A few hours he could tolerate, but a whole day? He pretty much liked everything about her except her need for discussing and analyzing everything.

Maybe what bothered him was that he didn't have that much experience with the nature of women. He'd listened to his share of fellows complaining about being henpecked. Every saloon he'd ever been in for the job had its share of husbands escaping to a so-called quieter place to think.

His mother had died giving him life and he had no sisters. Then he'd taken to the trail after burying his father. Gage never stuck around any town long enough to get to know a lady, much less court one. What did he know of keeping a conversation going with anybody, for that matter? He simply rode into a town, took care of his business and rode out, trying to leave it a better place.

He ought to apologize to Willow, he guessed, for not having gentlemanly ways. Those were skills brand-new to him.

Noticing the book of poems lying next to him on the bench, Gage lifted the gift and opened it. Had he thanked her or just put it back into the bag? He couldn't remember. It was thoughtful of her to buy it for him and he should've shown more appreciation.

Thumbing through the pages, he finally let the book fall open where it chose. The small print blurred before his eyes. Gage squinted harder, realizing with frustration that he was losing his ability to read faster than he hoped. He would miss it. Just as he had mourned the loss of writing down his poems. Now that part of him had to be buried and become only a fond memory.

Determined to at least enjoy one simple page of

the gift, Gage bore down and focused as hard as he could through the sunlit glare.

Suddenly Willow moved beside him, took the book from his hands, balanced it in hers and read to him.

"'Give me the splendid silent sun with all his beams full-dazzling…'" Whitman's words drifted like motes dancing among the rays in a sunlit window.

It was then Gage knew. Willow had somehow guessed he was headed into darkness.

A burden he had never meant to share with anyone.

Slowly, he took the book from her grasp and closed it. "Thank you, Willow. It's the finest gift I've ever received. I'll treasure it."

He didn't tell her he'd never been given a present from anyone but his father before. Even that had been a parent's hurried way of making amends for forgetting Christmas. Gage had gotten a handshake occasionally for a job well done or earned paid bounty for a man he'd caught and brought to justice, but he'd never received a gift just because someone thought he deserved one. Whether or not he would ever be able to read another word of the volume, he would keep it with him the rest of his life.

"Do you want to talk about it, Gage?" she asked.

"Whitman has a special ability to make you see what he does. Or better yet, he has the skill in choosing just the right words that allows a man to see something he's experienced in his own life. His words weave a different image in each reader's mind, I expect."

"I didn't mean talking about Whitman." She placed a hand on his as he held the book. "I meant do you want to talk about why you can't see the words well enough to read them?"

"You're mistaken." Gage stood and grabbed the now empty bag he'd brought with him, stuffing the gift deep into its burlap. "The sun was in my eyes for a moment. We have been facing east, you realize."

"Yes, and I also realize the sun is no longer directly in your face. It's long past noon. So you're saying there's nothing for me to worry about concerning what happened to you? That you've had a doctor check your sight for damage as well as what caused the scars under your eyes?"

Her concern pestered the daylight out of him. "Yes, I have, Miss Won't-Leave-It-Alone. Now, how about we gather all these ropes you've made, get you and the children fed and send you on your way back home before you upset Snow's day?"

Willow told Ollie and Thad to gather everything and put it in the buggy. The children grabbed all they could carry in one load and hurried off to do her bidding. After they were clearly out of sight, she turned and glared at him. "You know what, Gage Newcomb? I don't feel like taking a meal with you if you're going to keep treating me like some half-wit who can't tell you're hiding something from me and just don't want me to know what it is."

"Well, you know what, Willow McMurtry?" He couldn't contain his irritation. "The feeling is mutual. Why didn't you let me send that letter off for you instead of waiting and giving it to Junior Pickens to mail? Makes me think you might have something underhanded to hide."

"The mail? That's my business, not yours. And so what if I do have what you call *something* I don't care to share with just anybody?" Her voice rose an octave. "Are you some kind of Texas Ranger or marshal or other kind of lawman, ready to bust out your authority and haul me in?"

"Matter of fact, I just might be. Would that make you leave me alone when I tell you to?" he yelled.

"Uh-oh," Ollie exclaimed as she and Thad came around the corner and stopped in their tracks. "Maybe we better let Aunt Willow grab the rest of the stuff."

"Oh, I can leave you all the alone you want to be, Mr. Newcomb. I know someone else I can hire to teach me whatever I need to know from here on in."

"Don't know about you," Ollie told her brother, "but I think we better get back to the buggy."

"I'm with ya," Thad said, and both turned and sped around the corner.

Gage wished he and Willow hadn't argued in front of the children, but it was too late. The damage was already done on several counts. "It's settled, then," he told Willow. "You don't need me anymore."

"Not one minute longer."

"Then let me give you one last piece of advice. This one is for free." Gage's heart pounded as if a herd of buffalo had just trampled over it. "Don't worry about how you look in the eyes of others. People see you how they want to. That's the biggest lesson you need to learn. Find your own sense of worth in yourself."

They both stood there seething with anger. Neither willing to give an inch.

"Ready to pay up?" he finally demanded.

Willow started furiously digging in her skirt pocket.

"Not that." His voice lowered as an image sprang up clear in his mind. If this was the last time he would lay eyes on all that was Willow McMurtry, only one kind of memory would do. "You said I could ask what I want."

He closed the distance between them and encircled her with his arms. "I want this."

Gage dared to take the liberty of the kiss he'd forced himself to withhold for three days now.

At the precise moment his lips touched hers, all kinds of ringing echoed inside his head like a dozen cooks clanging iron triangles to beckon him from the field.

How long he'd roamed the boundaries he'd set for himself, thinking he belonged nowhere. To no one but himself. Yet amid the rush of emotions spurring inside him now, Gage discovered the true trail home lay somewhere within Willow's arms.

When his hands slid up to delve into those glorious strawberry-colored curls, her eyes opened and she sucked in a breath, ending their kiss. Instantly, a feeling of discontent settled over him, making Gage angry at himself for making such a foolhardy mistake and ignoring the caution that had warned him never to kiss her.

Now it was too late.

She would resent that he'd taken that one liberty and he would never be satisfied to walk away from her as she demanded.

As he must.

For he would never ask her to hitch her wagon to a blind man's.

It was a price he could not allow her to pay.

Only God could give him the strength to do such a thing, and he wasn't sure if this promise he'd made to himself was his will or the Lord's.

Chapter Twelve

The children kept their excitement about what they'd learned that morning between the two of them, giving Willow time to collect her emotions on the ride back to Daisy's. She knew they'd seen the argument between her and Gage but hoped they hadn't witnessed the kiss. That would only have left them confused, as it had her.

Tears lurked behind her eyes, her chest gripped with an ache so fierce she wasn't sure she could endure any more. If a stomach could be tied up in knots, hers was roped tight.

Neither child asked a single question about what had made Gage ride away from them without another word.

She was glad of that. She couldn't find the words within her to speak now, and she arrived at no real answer to give them. For today she sensed she had opened her mouth one time too many and possibly made the biggest mistake of her life. One that might never be repaired.

When they finally pulled into the yard, Ollie and Thad grabbed the makeshift ropes and Willow's bag, then ran into the house, leaving her to put away the team. She didn't try to call them back to help, instead climbing out of the buggy and leading the horses toward the stalls. Maybe unhitching the horses and getting them fed and brushed would keep her busy enough not to think about Gage.

Shepard Hutton appeared at the barn door. "I'll take care of those for you, Miss McMurtry. You look a bit frazzled. The kids do you in again?"

She handed him the reins, grateful that he had taken the task from her. She wanted to rush inside the house and bury her face in her pillow and cry. But whatever Shepard read in her face, she wouldn't let him think it was Ollie and Thad's fault. "The children were really sweet today. They didn't try anything sneaky this time, and we had fun learning how to make ropes. I'm just tired."

And she was. Tired of making one mistake too many. She shouldn't have pried into Gage's affairs. Admitting his lack of eyesight was his decision. If his pride was more important than facing the truth, then so be it.

When one of the horses shied slightly from Shepard's touch, Willow noticed the wrangler's hand shifted to the bullwhip in his holster.

Surely he wasn't going to use it on the animal.

Remembering how he'd cracked the whip to keep those other teams departing at a steady pace after the wedding, Willow didn't doubt he was proficient with any way he intended to use it.

"You've probably got lots more to do for the evening," she said, changing her mind about leaving the horses to his care. "I'm not too tired to put them away, and besides, I owe it to them for a fine journey. Brushing them down will soothe me and them." She reached to grab the reins from him.

When she accidentally touched his glove, Shepard's hand jerked away. His green eyes hardened as if turning to stone, the jaded glint warning her to back off. Freckles across the bridge of his nose boyishly opposed the flare of a well-aged temper.

She didn't back up, instead strengthening her grip on the reins.

He held up both palms as though she'd pointed a gun at him. "Was just trying to save you the trouble."

The fact that she'd never seen him without gloves made Willow wonder if there was a reason why. Had he hurt his hands in some way? Was that why he'd reacted so harshly when she'd touched him?

Shepard had been working every time she'd seen him. Nothing unusual about a top hand wearing gloves while he worked, was there? Was she just trying to find an excuse for his abrupt reaction?

Maybe she ought to rethink the possibility of asking him to replace Gage as her tutor. If he was that quick to fire up, how would he be when she made numerous mistakes? She learned faster and better from someone with patience.

Petting the horse that had riled the wrangler, Willow silently reassured the animal she would allow no one's ill temper to harm him.

She started unhitching the team, thinking Shepard would go about his business and leave her alone if he saw that she was done talking with him. Instead, he chose to move to a corner where he must have been oiling tools on a makeshift table that stretched over two barrels. Alongside the tools rested a brush and a can of something she couldn't define from here. Something black dribbled down the can's rim and darkened the bristles of the brush from its original shade. Leather polish? Boot polish, maybe?

When he turned to find her staring, Shepard swung back and went to work.

Just as she should be doing, she decided, instead of speculating what was so important to get done that he would not let her work alone in the barn.

It took her longer than expected to back the buggy into a stall because she didn't have enough strength to move it far by herself. Now that she realized how heavy such a conveyance was to move, she couldn't imagine how much harder it was to align a wagon by its tongue. She sure could have used someone's help about now and wondered if the other wranglers were out in the pasture taking care of the rest of her brother-in-law's horses.

"Next time you might want to back the buggy in first before you unhitch the team."

Shepard's advice mocked her effort. She noticed him staring at her now, a grin splitting his face from ear to ear. His gold tooth was missing. Had she only thought she saw one when she met him? Or was it one of those that could be removed for cleaning?

"Next time you might be kind enough to offer your suggestion before I make a fool of myself," she retaliated, wiping the back of her hand against her brow. She'd worked up quite a sweat.

She glanced at the table where he'd been toiling. No sight of a tooth on its surface, but the brush and can of whatever had been there were no longer in sight. Had he finished with them?

"Here, let me help you do this, at least. Then you can brush down the horses all by yourself." He lent a hand and with his added strength they managed to finally settle the buggy into its proper place.

She dusted her palms free of dirt, then started to offer him a handshake, stopping short as he took a step backward. She'd made the offer on purpose, wanting to see if it would anger him, as it had the first time.

It would have. He didn't want someone touching his hands.

Her writer's instincts kicked in and she felt a full-blown need to research the man. He was definitely hiding something.

Maybe even a gold tooth.

The world was suddenly full of secrets, it seemed.

She needed to know if Shepard had anything to do with the thief Gage was looking for and what danger or cost that posed for her family. Was he in cahoots with the criminal? He certainly had all the necessary skills to be of help to a horse thief and could too easily access a herd of valuable horses. Or could he be the actual thief himself? That would explain the tooth Gage mentioned and the one she was certain she'd seen gleaming on the day she'd met Shepard.

A bead of perspiration trickled down the wrangler's temple, leaving a strange trail of black.

Willow started to say something about it but a sense of caution filled her. Making him aware that she'd noticed it might not be such a good idea. Could the fact that he was sweating black droplets and had suddenly stored away the hairbrush and stained can have anything to do with each other?

She decided to keep quiet. Until she could find out for sure what was in that can.

Maybe Gage had reasons why he'd chosen to stay silent at times and she'd pestered him when she shouldn't have.

Maybe this was a fine lesson in learning when to be smart enough not to open her mouth.

And maybe by doing so, she would get the answers she needed regarding Shepard Hutton.

"After I finish brushing the horses, would you mind showing me what you're doing with those tools?" she asked, pointing to where he'd been working. "I'd like to see how and why you do some of the things you do around here. I'll pay you extra for showing me. I want to be better help to Snow when you decide to move on."

"Who said I'm moving on?"

"No one," she assured him. "You just have that look about you that says you don't stay anywhere long."

The past dozen days had been miserable for Gage. Though he and Willow were still at odds with each other, he'd made a point of keeping watch over her while she and the children were in town and particularly when her top wrangler traveled with her on the days she chose not to bring them.

Like today.

Shepard Hutton had apparently become the person she'd chosen to take his place as teacher. They rode in together on horses rather than in the buggy she used when the children were along. Both horses looked winded and her and her employee's faces were flushed as they dismounted at the mercantile and hitched their mounts to the rail. They went inside together.

Noticing Willow had been careful to make sure she remembered to tie the reins, Gage was filled with a sense of pride. He'd taught her that bit of precaution and he knew she would pass it along to others in the writing she created, maybe even saving someone's life someday. Possibly even hers.

Wondering if she'd been racing her horse for fun or had a more serious reason to seem in a hurry, Gage left his horse at Bear's hitching rail and followed her into the store.

The pair were in the aisle stocked with men's wares and clothing, talking to Junior Pickens. The merchant thumbed through a row of leather gloves and handed a pair to Willow.

She slipped them on and laughed at the size, holding her fingers up to show how the gloves swallowed her hands whole. "Too big. Better make it a couple of sizes smaller," she said, giggling.

Good, Gage thought. She wouldn't have been laughing if anything had been amiss back at the ranch.

Hutton leaned past her and grabbed a pair as she took off the first choice and gave them back to Junior. The wrangler opened one of the smaller gloves and slid it over her now bared hand. He did the same with the second.

"That better?" Shepard asked.

Gage didn't like the easy familiarity that had formed between Willow and her tutor since the falling-out *he'd* had with her days ago. He had no right to be angry about it, but he was. He'd known men jealous of their women. Every lawman worth his salt dealt with that crime. But he'd never understood its driving force until today. He was actually envious of the man placing gloves on Willow's hands. This new sense of possession toward her could become a danger if he allowed it to eat him up inside.

It was beginning to be a pain in his gut every time he saw Willow with Hutton. He almost wished he had another reason to chase the wrangler off. But so far, he'd found nothing to justify running Hutton out of the territory. And he'd searched hard. If the man was any kind of criminal, he hid it well.

Jealousy was a pit of bile Gage wanted no part of feeling. He had to honor her wishes and stay away. Had to remember his own reasons for keeping Willow's future clear.

Two women strolled in, greeted Willow with a friendly "How are you today?" and swept past her to the bolts of cloth.

Things had turned a corner for her here in High Plains. Willow seemed to be thriving with Hutton's help and was gaining respect from some of the locals. Deeds she attempted to make up for mistakes she made were the talk of the town now, though she tried to keep her kindnesses secret. Watching her so closely, Gage learned of them almost on the same day the repayments happened, and within hours, others' speculation always ended in fact with her name involved.

On Sunday the merchant and his bride-to-be even sat next to her and the children in the family pew.

Willow was blossoming without him and with the wrangler instead, finding a sense of worth in herself and respect from others for her goodness of heart.

Gage wanted to blame Hutton for being by her side as she experienced those changes, but it was his own fault he couldn't be the one celebrating with her all the things she'd worked so hard to achieve.

He had lived so long on the edge of life, like a lone wolf stalking its perimeters, he hadn't even known he was already mired in shadows long before his eyes were damaged and he met her.

Their time spent together had taught him that taking the opportunity to get to know someone, spending small moments that seemed as if they had no worth, filled him with a lightness and fullness of heart he'd never known existed. He wanted to experience more of the same and had no clue how he would ever live without that fullness, or her, and still remain sane.

Watching another man bask in the glow of her goodness, her friendship, whatever her heart cared to share, would be the sight that cast him into a darkness more blinding than the one he faced.

A yearning deep and consuming urged him to close the distance that separated him from Willow and let her know that he still cared how she was coming along. He didn't have to resume teaching her, but he hoped she would allow them to at least be simple acquaintances before he headed off somewhere alone one day.

Gage moved toward her, thumbing the rim of his hat. "Hello, Willow... *Miss McMurtry.* I see you're out early this morning. The children are both fine, I hope? And your sister? She and Myrtle doing well?"

"Fit and sassy, all of them."

Those eyes that seemed to warm his soul every time he gazed at them diverted from his and focused instead on the gloves she was removing from her hands.

"Ollie and Thad said to tell you howdy if I saw you," she mentioned. "I've seen you around town a couple of times but you never approached, so I didn't bother you. Wasn't sure you'd appreciate being disturbed."

So she'd noticed him watching, probably sharpening her powers of observation for her writing. That would serve her well, and it pleased him that she cared enough to be on the lookout for him.

"I've noticed you writing in your journal a lot. Do you have it with you today, too?" Gage tried to make conversation he knew she liked, but it sounded stiff to him.

Her companion shifted his feet, looking as though he was anxious to leave and ready to send Gage on his way, too.

Gage would have preferred not talking and instead simply taking Willow in his arms to plant a kiss on her beautiful bow of lips. But she preferred talking and that was what he intended to give her.

Bow of lips? Poetic words that raced to mind when he thought of her and only served to make him feel more miserable. He had to stop thinking like that.

Matter of fact, he had to stop talking to himself so much in his head so he could find a quiet place again.

"I left the journal in the saddlebag for now." Willow nodded toward the doorway. "But I've had a lot to write about. I even wrote a couple of poems I'm proud of."

"You seem to have things to talk over," Hutton said and tipped his hat to Willow. "I need to check on something over at the saloon. I'll meet you back here in about, say…ten minutes or so. Then we'll head over to the Rafford place and see about those horses."

His chin bucked toward the gloves. "Those are a good choice for the job."

Hutton bid the merchant goodbye but didn't include Gage. He strolled out the door, the chink of his spurs echoing on the wooden floor.

"What job?" Gage wondered aloud as she took the gloves and told the merchant that was all she needed.

"Not that it's any of your business anymore," she said as he followed her to the counter, "but he's going to show me how to choose good horseflesh to buy. He says I need a good pair of gloves if I'm going to handle horses that haven't been broken yet."

Gage didn't like the sound of that. Too much danger involved. She might have enough knowledge to be sufficient in riding a tame horse, but she was too green to deal with bucking broncos.

"Your brother-in-law gave him money and permission to purchase more while he's gone?" That seemed odd to Gage. He waited for her to pay for the gloves and put them on, then stuff the ones she'd worn from home into her riding skirt.

She shrugged when she finished. "I suppose the fact that he's doing this in my company means Bass did. I don't know the specifics of the agreement between them. Why? Do you think I should question him about it?"

The edge in her voice made Gage wonder if she was keeping something from him. His gut instinct kicked in. "You know something about the man, don't you?"

Her eyes glanced at the remaining people in the store before she spoke. "Let's head outside. I'll wait for him out there."

Gage reached out for her elbow and guided her as they walked alongside and was glad when she didn't shirk from his touch. He pointed to the bench just to the right of the door, shaded by the storefront eave. "This okay?"

She nodded but hurried to her horse instead of instantly sitting, pulled out her journal, then brought it back to hand to Gage. "If he looks out of the saloon, he'll think we're just talking writing."

Gage accepted the journal and asked her, "Why don't you trust him?"

"Take a look at the last seven or eight pages. You'll see."

Gage flipped through and found where the writing ended, then backed up eight pages. It seemed she'd been doing a character study on Shepard Hutton. The one statement that caught his attention first was the missing gold tooth and her speculation about it. "You never mentioned you knew the man had such a tooth."

"I wanted to make sure I wasn't mistaken before I told you about it, because I knew you would wonder why he kept that fact to himself when you described the horse thief."

"Anything else particular bothering you about him?" Gage thought about Hutton's ability with the bullwhip that day. It took a master of the craft to know exactly where to crack it without causing any harm.

She leaned over, giving him a whiff of how good she smelled. Gage closed his eyes for a second and savored the remembered scent.

"Turn the page and read that." Willow did it for him. "I think he's using boot polish to color his hair. I haven't caught him at it to prove it, but when the man heats up, he sweats black. Didn't you say your thief was redheaded?"

"Yeah, Hodge is redheaded. Maybe a few shades darker than yours. How do you know how Hutton sweats?"

She elbowed Gage in the ribs. "I work with him, fool. Keep your mind out of the wallow. Quick, thumb over to one of my poems and let me read it to you."

Gage turned back until he spotted one, then slid the journal into her lap.

Hutton had emerged from behind the swinging doors of the Twisted Spur and was already halfway to them.

About the time he reached the steps that led to the mercantile, she started reading, although clearly not at the beginning of the poem. "…freshly broken sod. The man who never quit now had a heart-to-heart with God."

Willow slammed her journal shut and complained, "See there, Gage. It sounds too simple. I can't find the right words to create those images like you and Whitman do. It sounds so ordinary."

He realized the game she was playing. Making sure Hutton didn't catch wind of any conspiracy against him. "May I show you one more thing before you go?" he asked, then directed his attention to the wrangler. "Can you wait for a second or two, Hutton? This won't take long."

Hutton frowned. "We need to be on our way."

"Show me." Willow countered her employee's impatience. "A few seconds won't matter one way or the other."

"Stand up." Gage stood with her. "Hand that to me." He accepted the journal and laid it on the bench.

"Now turn around and close your eyes." When she did, Gage wrapped his arms around her and covered her eyes with his hands.

Her body stiffened a second.

"Don't worry. I'll only do this until your mind

takes over for me. Now bring up the image of something you've seen or want to see."

"All right."

She didn't relax as he'd hoped. Instead, she seemed to become more unsettled. "Tell me what you're seeing, Willow."

"Right now, a horse bucking me off."

Gage knew what stirred that image and would have laughed had he not worried about the same thing happening if she went with Hutton to Rafford's place. He needed to calm her. "Describe the horse."

"Sixteen hands. Ready to hop and pitch and rear."

"Not bad. Now dig a little deeper," Gage encouraged.

"I told you that's my problem." She reached up to remove his hands and he obliged. "I can't quite seem to get past the first layer. My descriptions just keep coming up full of sand. Nothing rock solid and certainly not hitting any kind of deep well."

"Sometimes the first thought that comes to you is the right one. Simple can be better, but if you aren't satisfied with it, dig deeper." Gage brought up the image in his own mind. "How would it feel to be on that angry beast?"

"Like I was riding bucking thunder." Her answer came quick.

She whooped with excitement, her eyes flashing open as she swung around to face him. "That's it, Gage. That's what I've been missing. I can make them *see* it, but I haven't made them feel it yet. Letting someone experience it as if it were happening to them instead of the person in the poem. Showing, not telling."

"Exactly."

She grabbed her journal and hurried to unhitch the reins of her horse. Hutton had already mounted. After stuffing her journal into her saddlebag, Willow stuck a foot in the stirrups and threw her leg over. She reined her horse in the direction of her sister's ranch.

"I can't wait to get home and start writing," she told them. "Thanks, Gage. You've been a big help."

"You still going to Rafford's with me?" Hutton nudged his horse in the opposite direction.

Willow shook her head. "I'll probably just get in your way. Go on without me. I'll send one of the other wranglers to Rafford's so you'll still have someone to help you. I'm sorry, but I wouldn't be able to concentrate anyway. My mind's on what I just learned. I want to let this sink in first before I learn something new."

Without bothering to thumb his hat at Willow, he dug his spurs deep into the horse's flank, making the beast bolt down the street.

Relief filled Gage. He was certain he'd somehow spared Willow from danger. The fact that she was willing to leave Hutton so easily was proof enough she had no part of whatever scheme he might be planning if he was the thief. Once she'd ridden safely out of sight, Gage decided to take a ride out to the

Rafford place and see if there was anything more he could find out about the man in question.

One thing for sure. If Hutton and Hodge turned out to be the same person, he would regret taking up residence near a writer full of curiosity.

The second thing? Gage needed to pay a visit to the doctor again and see how much worse his eyes had become.

He shouldn't have been so easily fooled.

Chapter Thirteen

Back at the ranch Willow chose one of the wranglers to substitute for her in helping Shepard. She didn't want to delay what he had planned because of her change of mind. Rather than putting her horse away, she let her replacement take him so no time had to be used to saddle another. Good thing she was tall and the stirrups didn't need to be adjusted for Shorty.

Eager to start writing, she hurried up the porch steps and into the house. "I'm home," she hollered, heading upstairs to change out of her riding skirt and don a fresh blouse.

Willow got halfway to the landing and stopped. She'd left her journal in the saddlebag. By now the rider was probably a mile down the trail.

Her enthusiasm deflated like a child's balloon that had just popped. Everything she included in her writing today would have to be by memory alone. Could she do it?

Trust yourself. Dig deeper, she could almost hear Gage's voice encouraging her. *Write the feeling, not just the sight.*

Could she find that instinctive source of creativity within her and trust that it could be good enough to meet the challenge?

Okay. Because of you, I'll try, Gage, she thought and continued up the stairs. He had become the one person she wanted to write for now. To meet *his* expectations. He believed in her. He was the only one who saw in her all that was possible below the layers of her insecurity. If she could reach that level of quality and satisfaction with her writing, then she knew she would become good enough to capture other readers' interest and her boss's approval.

She would finish her story this afternoon and feel confident enough to send it off to Biven and let it decide her fate with the newspaper.

"What are you doing home already? I thought you and Shepard would be gone a lot longer."

Snow's voice startled Willow. She'd been so deep in thought she hadn't heard her sister come up the stairs behind her.

Once she reached the landing, Willow faced Snow and waited until her sister finished climbing the stairs. "I decided not to go with him after all. I sent one of the men to help him instead."

"Why?"

Though she tried not to take any offense in the tone of Snow's voice, the question sounded like yet another challenge between them. "I'm going to write instead. It's my day to do what I want, isn't it?"

She didn't intend to stand there and have an argument about anything, so Willow headed toward her room and sat down on the bed to remove her riding boots.

"Yes, it's your day." A frown creased Snow's forehead as she followed, pulling out the chair at the reading table to take a seat. "Besides, the children are fishing with Bear and Pigeon. I told them they could spend the afternoon with the Funderburgs."

"So, I have most of the day off tomorrow, too?" That was good to know. Snow always found the need to mother her or be involved in scheduling her day.

Anticipation made Willow smile. The Lord had answered her prayer before it had even passed her lips. Having extra time was just what she needed. If she could get a fair amount of writing in the rest of the day, she could take Ollie and Thad to school in the morning and get her story mailed off in time to meet the stage.

Maybe she'd even look up Gage and tell him how he'd helped her. Maybe even see if she could convince him to visit the doctor about his eyes. What was the man's name? She'd passed the plaque enough times hanging outside his office—she should have been able to recall it easily. Thomason, Thomas, Tomlin? One of those seemed right.

If she and Gage could get along enough to still be friends as they had this morning, then the least he could do was agree to let a friend take him to a doctor. That was what friends did for one another.

Willow glanced up from unlacing her boots, only to find her sister studying her closely, as if she had something else to say. "Yes?"

Snow triangled her hands together and the edges of her fingers touched her top lip. "I want to let you know I'm going to town with you tomorrow when you take the children to school."

"No problem." Well, there went the visit to the doctor with Gage. Willow hated the thought of putting that off.

She didn't have to imagine the ride to and from town with Snow. She'd endured a similar one when she'd arrived in High Plains. Fifteen minutes of tension and stiff conversation if they talked at all. Maybe Ollie and Thad would have good things to say about their day at school on the way back. Thad might. Not so sure about Ollie.

"I thought maybe you and I could spend some time together. Have breakfast or lunch, whichever you prefer. Maybe even visit the hat maker." Snow's hands moved from her lips to grip the arms of the chair. "See what trouble we can get into together. Myrtle needs a day to herself and I thought we'd both get out of her hair."

Willow dropped both boots to the floor with a loud thunk that echoed her disbelief. It was time to be honest. "I thought you didn't like me. Didn't want to be anywhere around me. Couldn't stand that I'm not as perfect as you."

Something deepened the color of her sister's eyes for a moment before they darted away. The pain of truth she'd finally spoken aloud? Willow wondered. Well, let Snow know the same hurt she felt thinking Snow merely tolerated her because she was kin.

"You thought wrong, sis." Snow stood and moved over to the bed, taking a seat beside her. "And I don't want this bickering to go on with us any longer. I feel like it's way past time for me to set things right between us."

Willow shifted a few inches away, not trusting Snow's softer tone or her seemingly sudden change of heart.

"I don't just like you. I love you very much—" Snow touched Willow's arm "—and I admire you even more for daring to pursue your dream. It takes a strong will to never give up on what you want in life. I'm proud of you every time I see you writing. I know someday you're going to achieve what you're working so hard for."

The cold ice of her sister's rejection, which had chilled Willow for so long, started to melt. "Really, you believe I can write?"

"I know you can. You have it in you."

Willow faced her and allowed her sister's fingers to thread into hers as they had when Snow used to walk her along the shoreline, playing in the surf.

Tears welled up from some deep pool of yearning Willow had thought dried up long ago. "I haven't been the best sister," she admitted. "I'm sorry I disappointed you so many times in the past."

"You were the baby. Learning. I was your big sister." Snow gently squeezed Willow's hand. "It was my job to be an example for you. When Daisy married and moved to Texas, that left me to teach you how to grow up right. It wasn't an easy thing to take her place."

Imagining how hard it would be to replace Daisy in the scheme of life around here, Willow began to understand a little better some of her sister's rigidness. "So all of this yelling at me and criticizing everything I did was because you wanted what was best for me?"

Snow nodded. "Sounds pretty harsh when you say it like that, but it is the truth. I'm sorry, sis. I hope you'll forgive me and we can become better friends than we've been sisters for a lot of years."

Express the feelings. Willow imagined what Gage might say. *The depth of feelings inspires the truth.* Willow let the tears she'd been holding back finally fall freely. "How about we forgive each other and start fresh from here?" she suggested and let go of Snow's hand to hug her instead.

Willow held on when Snow started to pull back. The tears kept coming and she couldn't stop them.

"There, there." Snow patted her back. "Having a bossy sister might take a while to cry out. Take as long as you need."

Willow sobbed, letting the emotion swell, then flood through her. "I—I'm sorry. I don't know wh-where this is coming from. I'm really very happy. Having one of the h-happiest days I've had in a long time, as a matter of fact."

She leaned back and looked at her sister's concerned expression. "Today I discovered exactly how to strengthen my writing. Now you like me again." Willow half gulped, half giggled. "And Gage, well, he and I are finally talking again."

Her laughter turned to a wail at the mention of his name and she threw her arms back around her sister and sobbed, "I couldn't be hap-pi-er."

Snow let her cry a few seconds longer, then gently pushed her back and thumbed Willow's chin up so that their eyes met. "Look at me. Tell me what's happened between you and Mr. Newcomb."

Willow told her everything. About Atlanta. Each of them hiding secrets from the other that brought tension between them. About her and Gage's quarrel and how they'd avoided each other until today. Even the kiss they'd shared. She told her everything except that she feared he was losing his sight.

"You're falling for him, aren't you?"

She should have been used to Snow's directness by now, but Willow was startled by the answer that she had no hesitation in giving her sister. "Past tense. *Fallen.* I've fallen madly, deeply, don't-want-to-lose-the-man in love. What am I going to do?"

Snow laughed and took one sleeve to wipe the

tears from Willow's face. "You never have a hand-kerchief around when you need one."

Willow remembered the one she'd stored away to give Daisy. She'd give it to Snow now instead.

"You're going to go after him," Snow insisted. "That's what you'll do. Rather, I'm going to take you to him tomorrow morning and you're going to *show*, not *tell*, Gage what he means to you."

Determination filled Snow's face. "Denying your-self of experiencing the sweetness of love will only make your face sour like mine."

"What do you mean?" Willow asked.

"I won't allow you to make the biggest mistake I ever made."

The sound of a bullwhip cracking and horses whinnying with fear carried a long way. Gage could hear it louder than the drum of his horse's hooves pounding over the hard-packed road. Hutton was making a big mistake in using the leather strap that called attention to how well he handled it.

When he drew near the corral of Bull Rafford's place, Gage noticed the size of the remuda gathered in the rancher's stock pens. He did a quick count and studied as many flanks as his eyes allowed him to see clearly enough. Not many. What few were branded looked legitimate and not worked over. Most hadn't yet endured the burn of angled iron into their flesh. Maybe Rafford had bought and traded for some of the horses in the past week or so, but the rancher had far fewer than this not long ago. Had he done some mavericking? Was that why Hutton was here?

Quality horseflesh for a cheap price? Or had Hutton played a role in the rustling?

Gage wanted to tread with caution here. Make sure he had the right man before he made a move.

Hutton hadn't dismounted yet but was cracking his whip, stirring up and riling the horses. From the looks of things, he had no purpose for his whipping other than to show off for some thin woman sitting on the horse next to his and shading herself with a frilly parasol. From the back, Gage couldn't see her face, but when she halfway turned, he realized he'd seen her before, but where? Even a blind man couldn't forget such a prominent nose.

The wrangler sat in the saddle about the same height and depth as the horse thief. Gage tried to see anything else about him that might bring more recognition. Nothing.

His hair was black and he hadn't started sweating enough for Gage to see if it would stay that color.

"Hey, boss," one of the men yelled to be heard above the crack of the whip, "looks like we got more company. You expecting anybody else?"

"Nope." Bull Rafford made the corral fence sway as he stepped down from its lower rung, where he'd been watching the horses. His enormous barrel of a chest was enough to strike fear in any opponent, but the remnants of a bruised jaw and chewed-off ear said he'd tangled with someone recently and met his match. He walked toward Gage. "State your business, partner."

Gage had no beef with anyone but the horse thief. He was sore at himself for Willow possibly seeing the truth first. He'd finish the job, all right, and take Hutton to justice if he proved to be the man he was after, but there would be no sense of achievement in how lousily he'd gotten the job done or the fact that he'd put Willow at risk.

"I remember you," Rafford said. "You were here a while back checking on my horses. That fella you was looking for ain't been nowhere around here. Sorry."

The whip quit cracking the air.

"Good," Gage answered. "Thought I'd check back. Heard you had a bunch of new broncs. This particular thief likes to choose what no one's branded yet. He's no good at shifting the brand. Keep an eye out for trouble. I suspect he's pretty close and has already caught wind of your bunch."

"You a lawman?" Rafford eyed the holster strapped to Gage's hip.

"Don't wear a badge," Gage answered truthfully. Of course, if anyone looked in the hidden pocket sewn under his horse's saddle, he'd find the letter of authority signed by the governor and given to all Rangers to carry somewhere in their belongings. "Don't mean I won't see that justice is served. You got clear papers on these animals?"

"Why are you asking, friend?" Bull looked as if he might be ready for the next fight.

Hutton interrupted. "Settle down, Rafford. It's me he's checking on, not you. Newcomb wants to make sure I'm on the up-and-up with buying for my employer. I showed you the letter of intent already, didn't I?"

"Sure did. Parker's bought from me before and I recognize the writing. He's a man of learning and writes better than most. You calling this one a horse thief, Newcomb?"

"Not yet, but once I have proof, I might."

"Let it go." Hutton coiled his whip and put it back inside the holster. "Don't much blame him for trying to impress that pretty piece of petticoat. Just don't like it being at my expense."

"What petticoat?" raged the thin woman. She jabbed the parasol at Hutton. "What did I tell you about taking up with another woman if you were courting me? I thought we had an understanding."

The wrangler's hand reached for the whip, then halted as Gage cleared the gun from his holster.

"Might be wise to reconsider," Gage warned.

The big-nosed woman reined her horse around, her eyes ready to spill tears. "Will you take me back to town, sir? I prefer not to share his company any longer. And to think I did… Well, I did things I've never done for any man."

"Sure, I'll be happy to see you safely home, Miss…?" What was her name? He didn't need or want to hear any more of her explanation. The fact Hutton had been paying court at the same time to two women, one of them being Willow, was enough to gall Gage. He ought to just shoot him on the spot.

But he wouldn't let jealousy rule his reason. He only hoped Willow's reason for allowing the man so close was merely to do research.

"It's Miss Finchmeister. Ellie. I met you at the Parkers' wedding, if you'll remember. My aunt's a founding member of High Plains." She sniffled, then started to wail. "I thought I'd found the love of my life. But he took me for a complete fool. How am I ever going to live this down, or tell my aunt, for that matter? I'll never trust another Texan as long as I live. Oh, except you, of course. I want to go back to Atlanta, where men are civilized."

Atlanta? The origin of the letter Willow had received on the day she arrived. Did the two women know each other well?

He wanted nothing more than to get this woman where she wanted to go and warn Willow and her family that Shepard Hutton was not to be trusted any longer. Whether or not he turned out to be the thief Gage was looking for, their employee was no kind of man to have around the place. If he himself had to stick around and take care of the ranch and horses until Parker and his bride returned, then so be it.

He wouldn't let Hutton back on the property if he had any say-so whatsoever in the matter.

The only trouble he foresaw now was how to get

Ellie Finchmeister to stop talking long enough to let him think how to go about convincing them.

He couldn't believe anyone could outtalk Willow.

Chapter Fourteen

"Shepard's home," Ollie shouted from somewhere just below Willow's window. "You oughta see how many horses he brung. They look fine and dandy. Come out and see, everybody!"

Willow had been writing so long at her table that her neck was sore from bending over the paper and her legs ached from the crease the edge of the chair seat pressed into the back of them. She yawned and stretched, reluctant to leave her story. She was on the last page and couldn't quite get it right. Nothing seemed good enough to wrap up the impression she hoped to leave on the readers about Ketchum so they'd want to ride along with him on his next adventure.

Evening shadows filtered from the window and she'd have to light the lamp if she didn't want to ruin her eyes. They already were blurring just from the amount of time she'd spent making sure every word rang true.

"Aunt Willow, come on! You gotta see this. Hurry up!"

"Be right down," she shouted back but didn't move an inch. The image was right there in her mind's eye. Just the right word would bring it into full focus and send her fingers flying across the page.

What would Ketchum be feeling at this point? she asked herself, shutting away the world that surrounded her now and climbing into the skin of the character she'd come to know better than herself.

Ollie's hollering faded. The four walls that encompassed Willow disappeared and became a stretch of Texas wilderness that spanned the horizon for as far as the eye could see. The sizzling heat of the desert made her back feel sweaty and she scratched it on a corner of her chair, which suddenly transformed into a tall standing saguaro cactus as she swallowed against a dry, thirsty throat.

The words started to flow and she grabbed her pen, hoping to catch them fast enough.

His particular trail that led to perdition had been paved with good deeds. All he had left to give was a saddle and a whole lot more sacrifice.

Ketchum thumbed up his hat brim and looked beyond the sunset ahead. He had little hope, but he remembered a time when he had none.

There was always the land—Texas, stretching out as far as a man dared to dream and was strong enough to venture. He turned his back on all he'd learned and lost, knowing the one thing he'd carry with him forever—the will to start all over again.

The wilderness faded and with it the drought Willow had suffered with her talent. Amazed at the images she'd created that offered the feeling of Ketchum conquering something within as well as without, she knew beyond doubt that this was the true character she'd wanted to create all along.

This was her grandfather's kind of hero. True to his profession. True to the land. True to himself.

Tears blurred her eyes as she wrote "The End," folded the pages into thirds and placed them in the envelope she'd addressed earlier to her editor. All she had to do now was put it in the mail in the morning. She left it lying on the table for now, full of bright promise and future dreams.

"Aunt Willow, are you coming?" Ollie whined, sounding exasperated. "You said you'd be right here. We're going to miss it."

Snow showed up in the doorway, carrying a lantern. "We better get out there or she's going to throw one of those ropes she and Thaddeus have been making and haul you down there herself."

Willow enjoyed the sound of her sister's laughter

joining hers. "You're right. She's about as patient as you were at that age."

They almost skipped downstairs side by side, the lightness in their steps revealing the joy their earlier talk had given both. The lantern swayed as Snow jostled it, flashing silhouettes to and fro across the walls, reminding Willow of the many times they'd played shadow puppets with their hands. She couldn't wait for morning for many reasons, but spending the day with Snow was one of them.

Myrtle stepped inside the house just as the sisters were exiting, looking hard at them. "Something wrong with you two?"

Snow and Willow shared a glance and laughed. "No, why?"

"Well, this is the first time I haven't seen you ready to smack each other." The chignon at the top of the short cook's head shifted as she stared up at them. "What happened?"

Willow giggled. "I fell in love."

Snow grinned. "I remembered how to like her."

"I'm going back to my kitchen," Myrtle announced, "until somebody around here regains their good sense. Forty-some-odd new horses. Breaking horses in the near dark. What was the man thinking! And he says he's going to hire a couple of new men. More to feed. Y'all need to give me a day off or one of you learn to be a better cook."

"I volunteer Willow," Snow suggested. "She needs to research that old saying about the way to a man's heart. Might want to break out another skillet or two, Myrtle."

"Get out there and see to them children. I've got hungry men to feed. Now shoo, the both of ya."

Willow hurried along, ready to take a great big old bite of life again. The one she'd just finished putting on paper had emptied her and she needed to fill back up with new knowledge and fresh ideas. She'd sleep good tonight, having put that story to rest, but she wouldn't let herself take time away too long or she'd lose the pulse of creativity that felt as if it still throbbed in her fingertips.

"Can't wait to watch the men break the horses. I've never seen that done," she told Snow as they headed into the barn.

The corral and the field beyond were full of horses of every color and height. Roans, duns, bays, standard army issue. "Shine the lantern on that one." Willow pointed toward a massive coal-black horse. "Is that what I think it is?"

"A Percheron." Snow focused the light on the magnificent beast that most stage companies preferred to pull their coaches. "Shepard knows his horseflesh. Bass and Daisy are going to be more than pleased by his purchases."

"If they're still here when they get back," Willow muttered, scanning the stalls for sight of him. "Shepard, you in here?"

"He's out in the paddock." Thaddeus came around the corner and frowned, his thumb pointing over his shoulder. "Told me and Ollie we better get on back to the house and stay there. Said it was too danger-ous and we'd be in the way."

The boy's gray eyes rounded. "Ollie kicked him what for and said this was her place and he worked for her, so she could be anywhere she pleased. I fig-ured I better mind him 'cause he's bigger'n me and he doesn't like us kids much. But I just want to watch. I promise not to get in the way."

Willow consulted with Snow on the matter. Both agreed if Thad stayed close to the two of them, he'd be safe enough. Besides, the boy needed to at least watch what the men were doing. After all, he'd one day inherit part of the ranch and might have to know how to break horses himself.

"Shepard, will you come here a minute?" Wil-low waved him in as she tried to meet him halfway.

The wrangler snorted impatiently and marched toward her as if he was still perturbed at her for changing her mind about going to Rafford's place with him.

"This gonna take long?" he demanded rudely.

She guessed all good manners were off. Her chin lifted as she shot him a glare. "I'm going to let the children watch what you're doing, but you don't need to worry. I'll make sure they stay on the other side of the fence."

"You agree with her?" Shepard thumbed his hat up and stared at Snow.

Snow nodded.

"Your poison. Just trying to keep 'em safe."

"We appreciate that," Snow offered as Hutton glared at Willow one last time and walked away.

"Glad somebody around here does. Oh, and Willow." Hutton pulled up the bandanna he wore around his neck to cover his nose, making him look much like the bandit she suspected he might be. "Shorty gave me a book he found in one of the saddlebags earlier. It's lying on my table where I oil the tools. Might want to take it with you when you go in."

Her face froze, and she hoped she showed no sign of concern.

He'd obviously opened the journal to find out its owner. Fortunately, she'd written her name on the inside cover, in the event she ever misplaced it. He wouldn't have had to search far.

"My journal," she told Snow, who shot her a look of curiosity. "I loaned Shorty my horse and accidentally forgot it was still in the bag."

Had Shorty read all that she'd written and shown it to Shepard?

Or had Shepard read farther than the first page?

Willow got her answer when Hutton winked at her and turned around, pulling the whip from his holster and lassoing the air with a resounding crack.

The horses scattered, racing away from the possible sting of being too close for comfort.

God help her if he was the man Gage was tracking.

She couldn't write herself out of the danger she might have just put herself into for real.

"I've changed my mind, sis. I don't think I'll let the children watch right now. It's later than I thought and will be dark soon enough. They're both tired from fishing and I'm exhausted from writing. Why don't we all wait until tomorrow to watch the men work with the horses?"

"Aww!" Ollie and Thad complained at the same time. "We're not too tired. We won't get to watch them till we do our chores tomorrow. They'll prob'ly be done already by then."

"Or gone," Willow whispered so only Snow could hear. "Hutton needs to be long gone by the time we bring the kids home tomorrow if he isn't already."

"You've got more to tell me." Snow took Thaddeus's hand and let Willow grab Ollie's.

"I can walk by myself," Ollie grumbled. "I don't need no help."

"But I do. I'm a little scared and I need someone brave enough to help me think smart," Willow insisted. "You reckon you could walk me back to the house and stay with me a while?"

"Sure. You chickenhearted about something?"

"And you aren't?" Willow tried to build up Ollie's pride so she'd be more willing to help. "Just one thing. I've got to stop in the barn and grab my journal before we head into the house. It won't take a minute, I promise."

"Okay, if we hafta."

Willow hurried as fast as Ollie's little legs could manage. Though her sister had no clue what she was about to learn concerning Shepard, she must have sensed her urgency, for Snow grabbed Thaddeus up in her arms and took strides that ate up the ground in great length.

Reaching the barn and rushing to the two-barreled table, Willow spotted her journal and grabbed it quickly.

Alongside it, gleaming golden in the amber light of a lantern, someone had laid a golden tooth polished to a fine sheen and a can of black boot polish.

She got his message. Keep her mouth shut.

Her gaze darted to the buggy. How hard would it be to hitch up, and could she stop her long-legged sister quick enough to get the job done before Hutton realized what they were up to?

She had to get them all to safety. Including Myrtle.

Letting go of Ollie's hand, Willow whispered, "Run and tell Aunt Snow to come back. That I need her and Thad. And then go get Myrtle. Tell her not to argue and don't come out complaining about being in the middle of cooking supper. The two of you stay together and meet me out front as quickly as you can."

"Something wrong?" Ollie whispered.

"Only if you don't do exactly as I told you, honey." Willow hugged her close.

Ollie leaned away. "Don't get all kissy-huggy on me, okay?"

Willow released her niece. "Remember, as quickly and quietly as you can, meet me out front. All you and Myrtle will have time to do is be ready to jump in. I won't have time to slow down much."

Ollie pressed her forefinger against her lip and nodded, then turned to run out the barn door toward the house.

Gage's horse thundered toward Daisy's ranch as he prepared himself for an all-out confrontation with Hutton, assuming the wrangler and his helper had beaten him there with the horses. He didn't know how many of the employees were in on the deal, but he'd face them all if necessary.

It had taken him far too long to get Miss Finchmeister settled down and back to her aunt. But helping the spurned woman served a vital purpose in the long run.

Seemed the things she regretted Hutton making her do had everything to do with keeping her out of trouble with the law. She'd spilled the beans about aiding him in forging the counterfeit letters of intent supposedly signed by Bass Parker. Hutton presented a letter to each seller and all the seller had to do was present the letter to the bank. Parker was a respected businessman in the territory and his word was his bond.

According to Miss Finchmeister, Willow's brother-in-law had written one letter for his employee to use in the event an opportunity to buy more horses presented itself while he and Daisy were honeymooning. But Hutton had duplicated it with

Ellie's help and was buying up horses all over the county with Parker's money.

Now Gage had enough proof to warrant taking Hutton into custody for embezzlement—a fancier name, but he was still a horse thief.

The sound of pounding hooves coming up the trail toward him at a breakneck speed warned Gage to move so he wouldn't be run down.

"Get out of the way, mister!" A woman's voice echoed Gage's silent instinct of warning.

A runaway team?

He'd barely shifted into the prairie grass when a team pulling a buggy full of people flashed by him, veering dangerously to the right to make the turn to High Plains.

The two left wheels tilted high into the air, setting off screams from the passengers before settling back onto the road in a jarring bounce.

Willow and the children! Her sister and cook. He had to catch them. Slow them down before they killed themselves.

Commanding his horse to turn, Gage's heels squeezed the animal's flanks until the beast burst into a gallop. Gage's heart pounded as he rode hard after them. Everything depended on him stopping that team. The image of Willow's mangled body lying on the road frightened him more than anything he'd ever faced. His first thought was to fire a warning shot, but he feared it would only scare the horses and make them run faster.

He'd have to outrace them and hurl himself on top of one of the frantic animals. If he made one wrong move, he would end up buried beneath a stampede of churning hooves.

God, be with me, Gage prayed. *Give me sight enough to see. Not for me, but for them. Don't let me fail them. Don't let me fail her. Forgive my pride. I can't lose her.*

Seconds passed. All he could hear was the sound of his heartbeat thundering in his ear. Blood rushed through his veins to strengthen and tighten the grip he had on the reins. Inch by inch he passed the back of the buggy, the second seat, now the first.

The children's shouts echoed, but the force of the wind rushing past him made their words indecipherable. Finally, he reached the hindquarters of one of the team closest to him. The trail of dust behind the wagon almost choked Gage as he fought to tie the reins around the saddle horn, but he didn't dare veer off into the grass and risk breaking his horse's legs on the uneven ground.

Gage rode now without anything but his knees and boot heels to maintain balance and not fall off. Edging up the team's flanks, he leaned forward and unhooked his boot heels from the stirrups. The shoulders of all three horses now kept rhythm as they stretched their necks to gain ground.

Leap. Gage ordered himself to take to the air and trust his sense of timing.

Amid the billowing dust and the stench of lathered

sweat, he landed with a jolt so hard it took him a second or two to recapture his breath. Being unable to see through the thick cloud forced him to rely on his other senses. Choking and gasping for air, he took a fair amount of dirt into his lungs. Saying another prayer, he reached for the reins…and found them.

"Whoa!" he shouted, pulling back on the leather guide straps and trying to sit upright instead of being buried in mane that rocked against his face. "Easy there, boy. Easy."

"No!" shouted Willow from behind him as the horses reacted to his commands, slowing considerably. "Don't stop them. We need to get to town. Fast."

Gage took a moment to gather himself. Exhaled a few breaths to ease the pounding in his heart. "Just give me a second," he yelled over his shoulder. "Stop long enough so I can climb in beside you."

"Every second counts," she argued, reining the team to a complete halt. "They're coming."

"Hutton?" Gage hopped down and waited until Snow joined the cook and the children in the backseat. Then he climbed in beside Willow and took the reins. Flicking the team into motion again, he let his horse run alongside the wagon without tying him to the back. Gage gave the team rein enough to run if necessary, but he kept them at a controllable gait.

"Yes, Hutton." She offered Gage a quick report of all that had happened since Hutton had returned with the horses an hour ago.

Particularly troubling was the fact that the man

had been daring enough to leave the tooth and can of polish for her to find next to her journal. He was taunting her, daring her to stop him.

"Now that he's no longer trying to hide his identity, he's a greater danger to you," Gage warned. "You and your family need to stay in town somewhere safe until Hutton moves those horses. I expect he'll do that tonight now that he knows you're probably headed straight to the sheriff."

Gage told her about what he'd learned from the spurned woman.

"Will she be in trouble for her part in it?" Concern filled Willow's face.

"I'll talk to the judge and see if I can get her off easier. She's his usual kind of victim. Young pretty lady. Naive. Easy to persuade. I feared you might be his target, but you turned out to be smarter than he was."

He remembered his thoughts about Willow not sitting any saddle well. She'd managed to find a way good enough to ride Hutton into a corner.

"You're a Ranger, aren't you, Gage?" Willow studied his face.

He finally admitted it, unable to keep the truth from her anymore.

Willow scooted away from him slightly. Would she forgive him? Understand his reasons?

"I knew it," Ollie boasted behind them.

"I want to be one someday." Thaddeus leaned up

and stuck his head between their shoulders. "Will you teach me?"

"If I'm still around when you're big enough."

Willow's eyes met Gage's and held.

"Can girls be Rangers?" Ollie appeared next to her brother. "I'd make a better one than him any ol' day."

"You two sit back and leave them to their business." Snow's commanding voice made the two rascals obey immediately.

"We've learned Hutton's secret, Willow. You just learned mine. I think it's only fair that you let me know yours." Gage watched indecision wash over her.

While he waited on Willow to feel comfortable enough to tell him, he kept an ear tuned to the sound of any danger approaching from behind and was relieved to hear none. He suspected that Hutton wouldn't take time to chase after Willow and her family. His pattern was to collect the horses and take off as soon as he caught wind of someone who read his trail accurately.

It might have been a different story if any of these fine souls had been foolish enough to stay behind. Hutton could have taken a hostage. Willow had outsmarted him.

Willow had grown quiet, not answering him about her secret.

Knowing it had something to do with Atlanta, he wondered if she'd made some kind of mistake she wasn't proud of. "Are you and Miss Finchmeister friends?"

"Acquaintances only."

"She know about your secret?"

"I hope not."

"Anyone else know about it?"

"She shared it with me just tonight," Snow announced from the back. Her hand reached to gently press Willow's shoulder.

"But it's something you'd rather I not know?" Gage was hurt when she simply nodded. She didn't trust him. "Care to tell me why?"

"You might hate me. I don't think I could endure that, Gage. Not now. Not after all we've experienced together."

"I could never hate you, Willow," Gage whispered. "That's a skill I'll never take up, I promise."

He thought he saw a tear well in the corner of her eye. What had she done that was so horrible?

"Does it have anything to do with your writing? The reason you're learning all these new things?"

"Aww, Aunt Willow. Put the poor fella out of his misery. Ain't nothing can be that bad."

Gage felt the same way and was glad the child had grit enough to say it for him.

"If you two want to get past what hurts," the cook said, speaking up for the first time since he'd boarded, "the only way to do it is open the wound and let the truth pop out. It may take some time to heal, but it won't lie there and fester anymore."

"It all started with my boss at the newspaper in Atlanta where I worked before I came here…" Willow began, sharing the long and involved story behind her true reason for arriving in High Plains. It was as if a great floodgate of motivations burst, spilling her secret and justifying what she'd done.

She'd thought his being a Ranger would put her dream of succeeding in jeopardy, yet she had recognized that he was exactly the kind of man who could best help her achieve her goal. Though he had noted she acted guarded when they were together, he hadn't recognized he was being used, and that surprised him. She'd played him for a fool and he'd let her.

What hurt most was that she thought him incapable of understanding the sense of worth she needed. Willow so wanted to be good enough at something that she was willing to go to great lengths to achieve it.

The irony of it all was that he, too, had been on the same quest and hadn't even realized it. He'd hoped to maintain his sense of amounting to something as a Ranger. As long as possible. He refused to give it up and settle for a life less serving if there was any way to avoid it.

How selfish he'd been, isolating himself, letting despair blind him, mining the tragedy without finding some kind of closure to it.

"I hope you'll forgive me for not telling you sooner." Apology etched Willow's face. "It sounds so shallow of me."

"I'm glad you told me." And Gage was. He could see how they both might be able to grow from the mistakes each of them had made. The cook was right. The truth was out. Now to let the wounds heal the best they could.

"We have this one last thing to do together," Gage reminded her. "Putting Hutton behind bars. Then both of us can move on with our lives, Willow. I'd like to say goodbye now in case our trails don't cross again. It's been a pleasure getting to know you, and I hope we'll always think of each other with a measure of respect. I'd shake your hand if mine weren't full of reins."

She searched his eyes, looking as if she had something more to say.

He hoped she didn't, for all he wanted now was to seek a quiet place to gather his thoughts and find a way to seal away his emotions.

He'd grown to love her, plain and simple.

Now he had to find the strength to walk away from her.

Willow said no more until they reached town and she instructed Gage to take them to the livery. Emotions too big to deal with right now had to be set aside. Confusion. Heartbreak. And, if she admitted it, anger threatened to engulf her and shatter her world into a million pieces.

She had to keep herself together. Make good decisions and no mistakes. If she faltered, she might be forced to pay a price too high.

The first thing to decide was whether to put the family up for the night at the hotel or see if the boardinghouse had a couple of vacant rooms to rent. Either seemed logical places Shepard might look first if the man intended to come after them. So maybe that wouldn't be such a wise idea.

Besides, she'd just about used up her funds and wasn't certain she could afford the cost of one room, much less two, anywhere.

All she could figure was that Hutton had chased them only a while, maybe just to make her feel threatened so he could have time to gather the horses and escape instead of trying to pay her back for being too nosy. She sure hoped so. She wanted him long gone so he posed no danger to any of her family anymore.

And before Gage decided to take out after him on his own, as he'd apparently been about to do before he thought she was in trouble with the team.

"Where do you intend to stay for the night?" Gage asked, climbing down to open the livery door. "Got anywhere particular in mind?"

Would he share his place? Let them put blankets on the floor long enough to get some rest? She still had no clue where he stayed. As a Ranger, he'd probably chosen somewhere he could come and go easily. "I haven't decided yet," she said, "but I'd feel safer if it's somewhere Shepard's not expecting us to be. So that leaves out the usual choices."

"The Funderburgs will let me and Ollie stay here," Thaddeus said. "They got bedrolls we take with us when we go fishing. Pigeon doesn't feel so good sometimes and gets tired. She likes us to curl up beside her if we're tired, too."

Snow climbed out of the buggy. "I'll check with them and ask. Might be a good idea, sis. That way, Ollie and Thad won't have to miss school in the morning, and they'll be safely tucked away until we're finished with this mess. I'll tell Bear what's going on and ask him to take them back and forth from school just to make sure. And I'll mention that you're putting the team away here for the night. I'm sure he won't care if there's room."

Ollie piped up. "He let a whole bunch of us sleep in his livery one night. I bet you might could sleep there if you want."

Gage checked inside the livery and came out shaking his head. "Already full capacity. Spotted a couple of cowboys stretched out in the hay and I heard someone snoring up in the loft. Sounded like someone big enough we shouldn't disturb."

"Could be one of my uncles," Ollie suggested. "They sleep up there when they come to town and can't ride good enough to get back home. They snore real bad. I should know."

"How about the three of us women stay at Doc Thomas's office or Bernie's?" Myrtle suggested. "Both of them have some extra beds that won't cost us a penny, I'm sure. Maybe even a couch long enough for one of you long-legged beauts."

"Try Doc's place first." Snow frowned at the cook. "I don't mind a cot, but I refuse to use a slab at the undertaker's."

A smile split Myrtle's face, lifting at least one of her chins. She laughed. "Okay, so I was trying to spice up the night with a little flavor of adventure."

Snow took each child's hand. "Leave it for another time, Myrtle. It'll be funnier when we're all not so tired. Once I've got the children settled in, I'll look for you at Doc Thomas's first. If you decide on any other place, just leave a message with him and tell me where to head from there. I won't be long."

Willow ran over and hugged her sister. "Be careful, sis."

Snow leaned to press one cheek against Willow's. "You, too, Will. We'll get through this together and come out the other side of it better. Have faith."

Willow watched her sister and the children turn the corner and disappear from sight. Hopefully, Bear and Pigeon had enough room and keeping the kids would place no hardship on the couple.

She and Myrtle helped Gage put the team away in the livery, trying very hard not to disturb any of the current visitors or their sleep.

Gage's forefinger lifted to his lips as he pointed to the door with his other hand and signaled them to head outside. By the time they were all rounding the corner, she noticed her sister going into the doctor's office ahead of them. It was hard to miss her wealth of white curls even in the dark.

"Looks like there was no trouble with the Funderburgs taking the children," Gage noted. "Snow's beat us to Doc Thomas's."

"You reckon he's there?" Myrtle yawned, trying to keep up with their quicker steps. "I know we're in a hurry but y'all are taking two steps to my four."

Both Willow and Gage slowed their pace.

"I've watched him ride in at all hours of the night and be right back up at the crack of dawn," Gage admitted. "No wonder the man is thin as a broomstick handle. But he must be really good at his profession. I've only heard great things about him."

Willow hadn't had the pleasure of meeting the man yet. She sure hoped he was really smart about one particular part of his profession. Taking care of eyes. She'd already made up her mind—if the doctor allowed them to stay, she would make sure the man checked Gage's eyes.

She knew Gage would fuss and holler about it, but she was prepared to stand her ground if she had to. That was what a friend would do, and she wanted to leave High Plains with Gage knowing, without doubt, that she considered him her friend. Whether or not they could ever be anything else.

"Do we knock?" Willow asked as they reached the doctor's office.

"Just go on in." Gage grabbed the knob and

opened the door for the ladies. A bell that hung over the door rang, announcing their presence.

"I hope I don't have to listen to that all night," Myrtle mumbled, waddling in to find a place to sit. "I'll think Old Bessie's gotten loose and I have to chase her down again."

Willow hadn't even thought of the rest of the livestock they'd left behind. She expected Shepard would take every piece of horseflesh on the ranch with him. But who would milk Old Bessie and feed the chickens? She smiled thinking of Butler. Maybe Ollie's billy goat would run the man down and butt him to kingdom come. It would serve him right.

She had to think of something tonight to make sure that the animals didn't suffer. *Please, Lord, let Hutton be on his way or get caught quickly.*

Either way his trail led him, she knew Gage meant to be part of the posse.

The posse. The sheriff. She needed to inform him as fast as she could. "You reckon the sheriff's still up?" she asked, hoping Gage might know.

"I'll find him once you're settled in somewhere." Gage looked as if he was champing at the bit to be on his way.

"He's probably on his rounds about now," said an extremely thin man as he came around the corner, cleaning his spectacles with a white cloth. Snow followed closely behind him.

"Howdy, folks," he greeted them. "Miss McMurtry here was telling me about your troubles. I don't mind at all if you grab one of my cots in the operating room or the davenport over there to curl up on for the night. I'm blessed with some empty beds at the moment. Now, if it had been last night, you might have had to wrestle for them. Some of my more rowdy customers did a little too much Saturday celebrating."

"I don't need one," Gage informed him, glancing at the ormolu clock on the doctor's mantel. "Just wanted to make sure the women have a place to lay their heads."

"I'll take that little settee over there." Myrtle pointed. "Me and it look like we'll fit fairly well together."

The physician settled his spectacles on the bridge of his nose, but they slid to a point just below his cheekbones.

"Where will you sleep?" Willow asked Gage, sensing his eagerness to leave.

Doc Thomas spoke up. "Still sleeping in the last pew over at the church?"

Gage nodded. "Just costs whatever I got for the collection plate. Warm. Safe. Open night or day. Clean to a fault and easy sleeping."

Myrtle's eyebrows rose as she sat on her bed-to-be and pressed her hands against the padding to test its comfort. "Does the preacher know you live there?"

"Yes, ma'am. In fact, he's the one who puts a blanket and a pillow out for me each night. I'd suggest you all grab a pew, but another fella sleeps there. Didn't seem right to bring it up."

The cook smiled. "My kind of man, the preacher, and you're free to tell him I said that, if you like."

"I will." Gage turned to open the door.

"Wait a minute," Willow said, reaching for his hand to stop him. "You wanted to see the doctor?"

If looks had the power to peel, she'd have just been skinned. Fury set Gage's features as he glared back at her and didn't allow her contact. "Leave it alone, Willow. Leave *me* alone. I've got things to do and places to be."

Confusion plowed a furrow on Doc Thomas's forehead as his eyes studied Gage's scars. "I don't mind, son. No trouble at all. Like I said, it's been a fairly easy night. You out of the salve I gave you for your face?"

"It's his eyes, Doctor." She dared to cross the line Gage had drawn in the sand for her not to step over. "Not the flesh."

"Follow me." Doc turned to head back down the hall from where he and Snow had emerged.

Clearly, Gage had wanted to leave, but he didn't. Instead, he simply stood at the door, seething at the choice she'd made for him.

Finally, he slammed the door shut and walked past her. "This is my business alone."

"Maybe once you're gone from here, Gage Newcomb," Willow countered, following him down the hall, "but as long as you're near me, I'm making it mine. I care about you."

"Don't. It'll get you nowhere. I told you. I can't love you. I won't love you."

She decided she was going to fight him all the way if she must. No matter how stubborn Gage became. Whatever was wrong, she knew his anger was really an echo of fear. Better to know exactly what she had to help him face.

Lead me, Lord, she prayed as she entered the room the doctor had chosen. *Give me the right words, the right advice to convince him this is the right thing to do. If it's what I fear and he's going blind, help me assure Gage that he still has a decent future ahead of him. These will be the most important words I've ever spoken and, Lord, You know how many have come out of my mouth. Don't let me foul this up. Let me dig deep enough to make him hear, help him see, let him feel and understand that I truly want what's best for him. Let this serve no other purpose but to set him free from what he fears.*

Chapter Fifteen

Anger consumed Gage as Dr. Thomas peered through the glass instrument and asked him questions. He'd been through this all before and it served no purpose now. The man would just tell him what he already knew, not what he wanted—no, *needed*—to know most. How much longer would he see? Was there a point where his eyes would ever stop getting worse or would they experience total darkness?

"Tell me again how this happened." Doc Thomas leaned back and switched off something that looked like a bright light fastened to a miner's hat. "Don't spare any details."

Gage glanced at Willow sitting in a chair next to the cot he sat on while the doctor examined him. She'd dug in deep and appeared unmoved by his deliberate anger toward her. She could be stubborn, mule-headed or whatever-she-preferred-to-label-it persistent, particularly if she thought she was right about something. And Willow was right about making him do this.

He'd thought about visiting a doctor again after she'd had to read Whitman's poem to him. He'd known then his eyes had taken a turn for the worse.

Gage had convinced himself he wanted to know how long, how much, exactly when to expect whatever would occur. But faced with reality, he was afraid of really knowing. Of accepting his fate without knowing whether or not there was still an ounce of hope.

He did his best to make the retelling short, accurate and to the point. He knew Willow was listening hard, waiting to hear all he'd kept from her. "I tracked a man. In an effort to escape, he managed to throw a bucket of wash water in my face. The water was filled with lye. As you can see, my skin's pretty much healed, but my eyes didn't come out so fortunate. A doc down south in Laredo and another in Fort Worth both told me I'll probably go blind. I'm hitching my hope to the prob'ly."

The physician nodded. "Looks to me like spectacles are in order for now. Not just any pair. They'll be pretty thick, but they'll help for a while. I'd say you're losing details, aren't you? Can't spot little things, but you still see the big picture?"

Gage nodded as the man offered him the pair he wore. "Yours will be twice as thick as mine, maybe more."

Studying the eyeglasses, Gage tried them on

for size. He shook his head, attempting to ward off the dizziness that immediately made his head spin. "These are supposed to help?"

The doctor pulled out a drawer and thumbed through a box that contained several pairs.

"You and I wear different lenses. You're farsighted and I'm nearsighted. Direct opposites." He chose a pair from the box. "Here, try these."

Gage returned the man's spectacles to him and replaced them with the new pair.

"Well?" Willow studied him, her face etched with eagerness.

"They'll do." He refused to give her the satisfaction of learning the doctor knew what he was doing. Everything came into focus better as Gage peered through the choice meant for him. It couldn't be as simple as getting a pair of new spectacles, could it? The first two he'd tried months ago had ended up crushed in a fit of rage beneath his boot heel.

Willow stood beside him now, patting his back as though he were a little boy who needed soothing. She had not one inch of fear of how angry he was at her.

"You're going to wear these from now on," she stated matter-of-factly.

"Not in public," he argued.

Exasperation exited in a rush of air from her lungs. "That's when you need them most if you're going to continue working as a Ranger," she insisted. "How will you track anything if you don't wear them?"

"They'll make me look vulnerable…limited." Gage stood and thrust the pair back at her, further angry that the doctor now knew what he did for a living.

Doc might as well know the rest of it since Willow felt so compelled to spill his beans. "That's the whole point. I can't continue my profession, and I don't know what I'm going to do about it. Rangering's all I've ever done. Who I've ever been. I don't know what else to be if I'm not that. I want nothing else but that."

He hated to see the hurt on her face, but it had the effect he needed to make her understand she had to go away.

Doc Thomas closed the drawer and faced them both. "Looks like you two have things to talk out that aren't my concern. So I'm gonna go get the other ladies settled in. Mr. Newcomb, I can see your frustration and I hope you find some kind of way to work through the circumstances you're dealing with. I've heard fine things about you. But, sir, my advice to you is to wear those as long as they'll help. After that point, put what's left to use in a way you'll be contented and will make you proud of yourself."

He brushed a hand through his graying temple. "A doctor has to give up his profession one day, too, you know. Just as many of us must face the ravages of time or circumstances. It doesn't make us any less worthy of respect, does it? The sooner you come to terms with your level of sight, the sooner you'll find a happier way to live with yourself."

He headed out the door and left Gage and Willow to a silence loud with the truth he'd spoken.

"He said what I've been trying to say, Gage." Willow held his pair of spectacles. "Let me help you find a way to keep your independence and lead a productive life. For example, maybe you could tell me some of the stories you must have as a Ranger. I could write them down and send them off to my boss along with the story he's waiting on from…"

Her face turned ashen as she whispered, "Oh, no, I left the envelope on the table. I didn't think about it when I left ho— Oh, now what am I going to do?"

"What envelope? What table? What are you talking about?"

"Nothing important," she said, looking slightly dazed and full of a brand-new secret. "Nothing that can't wait until morning, that is. I think we're both tired and need to get some sleep, don't you? No use arguing this point any more tonight. How about we meet at the livery at the crack of dawn, grab the buggy and see if we can't wrangle up the sheriff and some men to help us flush out Shepard?"

"You can wait till morning if you like."

"Promise me you won't do anything tonight." She handed him the glasses. "It's dark and you'll see better in the morning. Handling Shepard and his men is going to be hard enough in daylight."

"I may be almost blind, but I recognize that look too well." Gage felt it in his bones. She was about to set something into motion and put herself at risk again. She was the one who needed to make a promise about staying put.

He only hoped whatever was troubling her had nothing to do with the horse thief. There was no room or time for mistakes where that man was concerned. And Gage wanted her far out of the way when he headed to Daisy's ranch to serve Hutton his final justice. Soon as he left and conferred with the sheriff, he'd be fast on Hutton's trail.

"Promise me you're not planning anything foolish," he demanded.

"When have I ever done something like that?"

"I want to leave here knowing that you can take care of yourself."

"Then you still won't stay, no matter what?"

She wasn't asking him to remain in town until morning. Willow meant forever.

He stared into the palomino eyes that had come to mean so much to him. He wouldn't lie. He couldn't. "No matter what, I'm gone once I capture Hutton. It's what has to be."

Chapter Sixteen

The children were safe in bed at Bear's, Snow and Myrtle long past asleep and Gage gone to, she prayed, his church pew. As tired as she was by the night's events, Willow couldn't sleep. She lay on the cot next to Snow's and was grateful her sister had started snoring. That meant whatever sounds she made in sneaking out of the doctor's office wouldn't awaken Snow.

Myrtle, on the other hand, would be the one to pass with caution. How in the world would she get past the bell that hung over the door without the cook's knowledge?

Sitting up carefully and hoping the wooden cot would not creak from the effort, Willow settled her boots to the floor. Fortunately, her sister had accepted the fact that she elected to keep her boots on in case trouble came during the night and they had to be quick about leaving.

A glance at Snow's feet stirred a moment of appreciation for her sister's support. Snow still wore her shoes, too.

Willow grabbed the blanket off her cot and tiptoed carefully out of the room and down the hall to the parlor. Just wonderful. Myrtle had left the lamp lit, or else the doctor had for whatever purpose he deemed necessary. A glance at the cook curled up tightly on the settee confirmed Willow's need to be especially careful in not waking the woman. Her little round body barely fit, and it must have been hard finding just the right position for comfort.

Now, how to cover the bell with the blanket so the ring would be muffled when she pulled open the door?

She'd been blessed with height, but even on tiptoe Willow wouldn't be tall enough to drape the blanket over the bell and stuff it between each side of the clapper. Everyone knew she wasn't exactly the most graceful person on earth, and she would be putting herself in a precarious position if she attempted it without help of some kind.

No footstool in sight anywhere.

Only a table in front of the settee where the doctor had left some copies of *Harper's Bazaar* for his patients to read if forced to wait. Most of his customers must be women. The year-old fashion magazine was all the rage in the East and she was surprised that its popularity had reached this far west already. Dare she try her weight on the table?

Over in the corner next to the locked medicine cabinet stood a pole with a covered birdcage hanging from its hook. Beneath that sat a burlap bag propped against the pole. Seeds? It looked full enough to add just enough height to make a difference.

Willow tiptoed over and checked the material that tied the bag closed. Her knowledge of rope now served her well. The rawhide was twisted firmly and secured the burlap adequately. Probably had to be tied strong to keep out little curious hands that liked to explore things while waiting and were eager to help feed the pet.

Hopefully, this would do the trick.

Willow tried to lift the bag, only to grunt with effort. Her eyes shot over to see if the sound had disturbed Myrtle. The woman wiggled for a second, yawned, then settled back into place.

Nothing she could do but drag it. The volume that would give Willow the added height she needed was far too heavy to lift.

She grabbed the rope end and began to pull, only to bump the table filled with magazines.

Grimacing, she readjusted her angle enough to slide around the table leg that had almost proved her undoing. Finally, gratefully, Willow managed to reach the door. Now to lay down the bag and get a good step up.

Thunk! It landed with a thud louder than she'd expected.

Remembering to grab the blanket again before

daring to maneuver herself into position, she lifted one foot and planted her heel firmly atop the middle of the feed bag. Testing carefully, she lifted the second.

Seeds shifted, making her wobble, and she had to stuff part of the blanket in her mouth to keep from saying, "Whoa!"

Her pulse bounced in her veins as if it were bubbles dancing in a pot of hot water.

She took the blanket from her mouth and reached up to see if she had enough height to get the job done.

She did. Stretching a length of the blanket between both hands, she balanced on the pads of her feet and threw the material over the bell. Momentum carried the blanket high enough, and she was able to stuff some of it around both sides of the clapper.

Done! She praised herself for a job well accomplished as she lowered her heels to regain a steadier surface beneath her feet. Her weight shifted the seeds again and she almost retwisted the same ankle she'd hurt the other day.

Great, that's all I need, she thought. *Hurt myself before I even get started.*

Afraid to linger any longer, Willow sucked in her breath, opened the door and looked up. The bell didn't ring. She exhaled ever so quietly.

But neither would the door open very far. She'd forgotten how heavy the bag was. Willow was afraid to scoot the door open any wider for fear that the movement might be too jarring and change the position of the blanket that kept the clapper silent. Would she be able to squeeze through this small opening?

Only one way to find out. She sucked in her breath again, this time as hard as she could, hoping to flatten her stomach as much as possible. She pushed her right shoulder and hip through, turning her head sideways so as not to bump her nose. Pressing her cheek tightly against the outer side of the door, she slid a little farther but seemed to get stuck. The left side of her body refused to mold itself to the effort.

Willow could just imagine somebody coming along and finding her in such an embarrassing position.

Suddenly somebody grabbed her right hand and gently yanked her from the side. She started to scream but couldn't. She could only expel the breath she'd sucked in for so long.

"Going somewhere?" a man's voice asked.

Doc Thomas! She'd thought he was asleep somewhere in the back of his office. What was he doing out here? How would she explain this without his hauling her off to an asylum?

"Uh…I…uh…got stuck, you see."

"Yes, I noticed that." He let go of her hand.

"Well, I decided I needed to go check on something important I left back at the house. I didn't want to wake any of you." She felt like a child confessing to a bad deed done, but she'd really meant well. "I stuffed a blanket in the bell over the door so it wouldn't ring and wake up everyone as I left. You'll see how I managed that when you go inside. But as you can tell, I had a little trouble achieving what I set out to do. I apologize for the mess you're going to find."

Doc Thomas nodded. "Apology accepted. I just want to know one thing."

She hoped she didn't have to reveal any more about the why of her actions. "Yes?"

"Why didn't you just use the back door?"

"Oh." She wanted to melt right there in the road into a muddle of stupidity. Who would have thought there was a back door? "Wasn't thinking, is all I can say."

He laughed. "At least you're honest. I'll let you go, then, and, Miss McMurtry, if you return and would rather not set off the bell, go around back and come through the kitchen. My office used to be someone's home before it became a business."

"I'll remember that," she said and hurried away as fast as she could before she died of embarrassment in front of him.

Gage didn't know how he'd managed to get here. Last thing he remembered was opening the sheriff's office door and finding the lawman sprawled over his desk. Rushing up to make sure the man still breathed, Gage had heard a plank in the floor creak under the weight of a heavy boot. Lantern light had played along the wall, revealing a shadow with an arm raised to strike.

Now Gage lay across a church pew staring up at the rafters high into the steeple tower as he fought the dizziness that blurred his vision. He tried to stir up the images lost after the crashing blow that had sent him hurling into oblivion.

With a moment of realization, he noticed daylight dancing through the sanctuary's stained glass window. Gage sat up, trying hard to focus. The wooden pew creaked as he shifted his weight, remembering.

Someone had muttered Willow's name in the moment before he'd been clubbed. A promise to make her pay. Then the crashing blow from a blunt instrument that brought nothing but pain.

Gage was surprised to wake up alive. If the person had meant to kill him, there'd been plenty of opportunity.

Vague memories floated back. Wondering if his attacker was a man or woman. He couldn't tell by the odd shape of the shadow or by the fierceness of the blow. He'd gotten up from the sheriff's floor. Accidentally stepped on the glasses that had fallen from his face. Stumbled to the church to gather his wits and more guns. Finally passed out on the pew.

How many people were still angry enough at Willow to want to hurt her? To need to get him out of the way, knowing he would stop at nothing to rescue her?

Hutton was the logical conclusion.

Aspiring brides in search of a bouquet couldn't be discounted either.

A spurned intended?

He had to find Willow, get a quick list of her enemies and hope that he had enough unscrambled brains left to protect her from all threats.

What was it she had said before he'd left her to head to the sheriff's office? Gage tried to concentrate. Maybe if he could clear his head long enough to remember their conversation, more of his memory of what had happened would come back to him and he'd know who posed the threat to Willow.

She'd forgotten an envelope. Left it behind. Did the envelope have anything to do with whoever had felt the need to get him out of the way?

Maybe all it meant was she was worried about something to do with her writing. Surely that had to be it. Her writing was all that had really mattered to Willow since she'd arrived in High Plains.

In the stillness, Gage heard an inner voice echoing through his mind and heart.

Not true. She cared enough to see you go to a doctor. Faced you down like a gunman, challenging you in the middle of the operating room.

And she didn't flinch, not once, at your stubborn refusal. Willow cares for you. Not just cares but loves you. And all you can do is insist that you're leaving her.

If Gage meant to get on with his life and quit pouting, it would take Willow's kind of grit and heart to see him through the changes. Instead of fearing he would become nothing but a burden, he was meant to glory in what they could be together.

Gage realized he'd been too blind to see what was staring him in the face.

He didn't have to live alone anymore.

Emotions that he'd only recently come to know filled him. Anticipation that things could get better. Longing for more and belief that he had a right to dream. Faith that he could put his many losses behind him and find a future worth living.

"Thank You, Lord," he whispered, bending to his knees and bowing his head, "for letting me see in time. For allowing me to survive this attack. Most of all, Lord, guide me straight to the person who means her harm."

Chapter Seventeen

Careful not to make a sound, Willow moved through the livery to reach the buggy. With Gage and Snow's help earlier, she'd managed to face the horses in the proper direction this time, and she didn't have to worry about harnessing them again. All she had to do was loosen the hobbles, climb aboard and be on her way.

It occurred to her that the ride would be faster if she took just one of the team, but then saddling and adjusting the stirrups to the right length would take up too much time. She would be forced to borrow all the makings from Bear's tack room and she wouldn't do that without him knowing. That would be nothing short of theft and there'd been enough of that around here already.

She would just have to chance making it out to the ranch and back in the buggy and hope no one became the wiser of her absence.

After removing the hobbles from the team's front legs, she stroked the animals and whispered a promise of extra oats when they returned. Willow climbed aboard and settled in the front seat, discovering her journal had lodged between the brake and the footrest. She was glad she'd had the presence of mind to grab it off Hodge's table earlier. She'd been so worried about the story she'd left behind in the envelope that she hadn't given the book a second thought until now.

The image of the last place she'd seen it made her shudder. Next to the tooth and the can of boot polish. Proof that Hutton meant to intimidate her.

Just as she retrieved her book, a *whoosh, whoosh, whoosh* broke the silence in the darkened livery.

A sharp sting bit her shoulder, then coiled around Willow so fast that the leather strap pulled her arms against her ribs as if to squeeze the breath from her. She felt like a rabbit trapped in a rattler's grip. Willow was jerked from the seat, only to land in the straw that covered the stall floor. Her journal lay next to her cheek now.

She did her best to scream, praying it would awaken the men Gage had said were sleeping in the livery. Or at least someone from outside. But she had to spit straw away from her lips, garbling the scream. No help came. Not even from Bear.

"Don't bother, Willow. Those men won't hear you or be up anytime soon. We made sure of that," chided a voice from the door she'd left open to give her quick exit. "And don't be counting on the blacksmith or your precious Ranger either. Let's just say each of them's gonna have a little trouble tracking for a while once they wake up."

"You better not have laid a hand on my niece and nephew or I'll—"

"You'll what?" Hutton laughed from atop his horse, backlit by the moon. "Kill me? Should have done it when you had the chance, lady. This ain't one of your made-up stories. The hero, or should I say in your case, the heroine, doesn't always get what they want in real life."

"If I get up from here, you'll wish you never laid eyes on me," she spat.

"Oh, you're getting up, all right, lady. I'm taking you back, using you for bait. Your Ranger's gonna come calling, I guarantee you. I'm gonna make him wish Ellie had gone ahead and finished the deed instead of leaving him for dead."

"Ellie?" Surprise filled Willow. She was in on all of this? "Who is she to you?"

"I had a change of heart since I talked to the Ranger. I'm going to be Mrs. Hutton." The large-nosed woman from Atlanta came around the livery door with a bandanna in her hand. Looking up at the wrangler, she asked, "Now, Shepard?"

He nodded and laughed. "Anytime you're ready, darlin'. Make sure you stuff it in good."

Willow struggled against her bond, jerking her head this way and that so Ellie couldn't cram the bandanna into her mouth. "Ask him what his real name is," she sputtered. "It isn't Hutton. Is it, Stanton? Don't be fool enough to trust him, Ellie."

The whip jerked and he backed the horse away from the door. Willow slid across the straw on her belly, picking up splinters from the boards beneath.

Did he mean to drag her all the way back?

All of this because she couldn't wait to get her story sent off. Because she feared she couldn't recreate it again. Because she'd allowed her need for approval to make her reckless and endanger the man she loved.

Willow closed her eyes, gagging against the dust that billowed beneath each hoof that gouged the trail in front of her. Suddenly the images and emotions rising within her became too vivid for her to hold back the fear. She began to pray and ask God to help her.

Don't let Gage find my journal, Lord. If he sees it, he'll think I'm dead. He knows I'd never leave it willingly. He won't stop until he finds Hutton and then it might be too late. He might not see the danger I've led him to.

Please don't let him die trying to rescue me.

I could never be worth that much.

To him or to myself if I lose him.

A little after dawn, Gage left Doc Thomas's office with his head wound looked after and his mind frantic with concern. No one knew where Willow had gone. Only that her cot remained empty. The physician admitted seeing her long before dawn and said she had told him she was going somewhere for something she'd forgotten. He explained the way he'd found her jammed between the door and its threshold and how he'd wondered why she hadn't thought of using the back entry.

Gage knew. She hadn't wanted anyone to hear her leaving. Only by happenstance had Doc Thomas come to her rescue and learned of her mishap with the door. Where would she have gone next? Too much time had passed.

He'd best check the livery. See if her buggy was still there. If so, he'd be relieved that she hadn't taken the foolish notion to return to the ranch and pick up whatever she'd forgotten. Nothing could be that important with the thief still on the loose and believing she had spoiled his racket.

When Gage found Willow, he meant to take her in his arms, beg her forgiveness and pledge his undying love to her. He would even admit that he couldn't— no, *wouldn't*—live without her.

Taking Hutton into custody would just have to wait. Telling Willow he wanted her in his future must come first.

As he drew closer to the livery, Gage noticed something had been dragged for a great distance from its door. The hackles on the back of his neck rose and his guts felt as if someone were twisting them into rope.

"Say, Newcomb," Bear hailed Gage as he came from his personal quarters. "You mind fetching the sheriff for me? Had some trouble this morning. I just came to. Found my wife and my fishing partners all tied up. I'd still be out, but Ollie and Thaddeus were able to unknot the ropes and throw a bucket of water on me to revive me."

"Trouble? Who was it?" Gage wondered if Willow had been anywhere in the vicinity. He needed to get into the livery and quick. "Sheriff ran into a little of the same thing himself last night."

"Believe it or not, it was a thin piece of woman with a big nose." Bear sounded astonished by the fact. "She was with Parker's wrangler. According to Tadpole and her brother, it seems the wrangler's out for blood, but it wasn't ours. We were blessed that the pair only seemed to want us out of the way."

"Have you checked your livery to be sure?"

Bear shook his bald head. "I was on my way just now to see if the cowboys who were sleeping it off for the night had fared any better than us." The blacksmith pointed to the disturbed earth Gage had noticed earlier. "Do you see that? Something's been dragged a ways past yonder. Sure looks long enough to be a body."

Both men broke into a run toward the open livery door. A path leading from the stall where Gage had helped put away Willow's team and buggy had been swept clean of straw. Seeing no sign of her, Gage wanted a better look at the stall itself.

"Check out your visitors," Gage urged the black-smith. "It's too quiet. There was plenty of snoring last night when I checked for room. See if any are still here. I'm going to see if I can tell whether or not Willow's been by this morning."

"Can't find her?"

Gage caught Bear up with what had happened and the fact that no one had seen her for hours.

Bear's voice came from somewhere on the ladder that led to the loft. "Man down up here. Two in the far corner on the other side of Willow's team. I'd say some big trouble happened here. From the looks of things, I'm guessing we were right in thinking that might have been a body dragged out the door."

"I hope you're wrong," Gage whispered as he spotted the journal lying in the straw next to the team. He picked it up, clutched it in his hand and set his jaw.

She'd been here, all right. And she'd never leave, on her own accord, without the journal. His worst fears were realized. Trouble had tracked her here.

Was she dead?

All seemed lost.

What a fool he'd been to dwell on a mere loss of eyesight when now he'd lost his heart.

The sun had brushed away the fog of morning as Gage watched from the barrier of mesquite bushes that lined the approach to Daisy's ranch and counted the men coming in and out of the barn. Not as many as he'd expected.

The other hired men must have already taken the horses and headed south to Mexico or west to mesa country, where they would rendezvous with Comancheros and the like. Why Hodge hadn't joined them baffled Gage. The man usually stuck around only long enough to strike and run as if he had a yellow streak painted down his back, preferring to be one step ahead of the law. This time, he seemed bent for revenge or a reckoning.

Well, let him come. Gage was ready for him. But the thief wasn't the sort to deal the cards fair. He always had a trick up his sleeve.

Hair on the back of Gage's neck stood on end. If Hodge had hurt Willow thinking it would draw him out, the man had made the biggest mistake of his career. He would answer for every pain she had suffered if she'd been the unfortunate soul dragged behind that horse. Gage didn't care how he took the man to justice anymore. An eye for an eye or in chains, it made no difference to him.

If Willow survived, she had to be inside somewhere among them.

Easy there, Gage told himself as his heart hammered in his chest. He had to tread cautiously now and size up the situation well or he'd just end up putting her in further danger. Gage prayed fervently he wasn't too late to make a difference.

He was glad now he'd convinced Bear to stay and

form a posse in the event the sheriff hadn't recovered enough to get this under control. Maybe they'd show up in time, but Gage wouldn't count on it. He vowed to catch the men on his own if need be.

About a mile out of High Plains, he had spotted signs that the dragging had stopped. Whatever the burden, it had been thrown over the mount in front of the rider and carried the rest of the way.

The evidence gave him hope there was a chance Willow might still be breathing.

Waiting until he was certain all the men were now inside, Gage crept closer and pressed an ear against the barn wall. No one bothered to lower his voice, proving none of them were afraid of being caught.

"Gage will tear you into tiny pieces for what you've done," Willow threatened. "You better ride, and ride hard, because he won't stop."

The sound of her voice weakened Gage's knees, washing relief through him like floodwater over land cursed by drought. All he wanted to do was bolt in there and commence to firing. But he couldn't. He might lose her for real this time.

His mind raced, wondering how he could cause distraction enough to give her time to run to safety. If she still had strength to walk. She seemed to have no problem talking, but he needed a good look at her. To see how badly she'd been hurt. Make sure it wasn't just pure grit that sharpened her courage.

Sweat beaded on Gage's forehead as his teeth

ground together. He had to do something and do it now.

"Hold it right there!" he shouted as he stepped inside with both guns pulled.

Hodge shifted out of the direct line of fire, taking shelter behind the chair where he had tied Willow.

"No!" she shouted, her hands and feet bound with rope. "He means to kill you. Get back. There's four of them."

Gage focused on her face for a moment, quickly raking in her beauty beneath the scratches, splinters and blood. She'd never looked more precious to him.

"Guess I'll just have to shoot two at a time, then," he assured her even though they both knew he would be outgunned.

Willow fought against her bonds, struggling to break free. "Don't do this, Gage," she pleaded. "This is exactly what he wants. He told me so. Told me he was going to use me as bait to lure you. I didn't want you to come. I hoped you'd see the journal and think I was already dead. That it was too late."

"You're mistaken, love. It's never too late for you and me. We're just beginning."

"Aww, isn't that just the sweetest thing you ever did hear," Hodge mocked. "The Ranger's lost his heart along with his good sense."

"I have no beef with you other fellows. Just Hodge here. He's run out of steam." Gage made sure he kept close watch on the other three. Each had a gun, but he didn't know if they had the grit to use it on a lawman. Rustling was one thing; most men had no stomach for killing. "I'm giving you a chance to change your future. Got a posse riding this direction. Should be here any minute now. You can take the time to try and draw on me if you want to test my mettle. But if you try it, I'm taking as many of you down as I can get off shots."

"I don't know about this, Hodge," one of the men said. "Kill one Ranger, you got the whole corps coming after you. I think I'll pass." He walked out the door leading to the paddock.

Three to one now. Gage liked the better odds. Now get it down to two. One for each gun.

"Come back here!" Hodge shouted. "You leave now, you lose your cut of the money."

"Leave that woman and let's get out of here," said another outlaw. "Posse's coming. She ain't worth this."

"If you're going," said the third one, "no reason for me to stick around. I ain't no gunman."

The sound of a bullwhip cracked the air, stopping Hodge's helpers from leaving. It snaked around Willow, making her scream. Hodge gripped the handle and pressed the end against her throat. "Put the guns down, Ranger. Slide them to me or I swear I'll squeeze this until she squeals."

"Don't, Gage. It's not worth it. I'm not worth it."

"You're worth everything to me. Don't ever let me hear you say such a thing again. Do you love me, Willow?" Exasperation filled Gage.

Her eyes rounded. "Of course."

"Then will you please do something for me?"

"What?" Hodge asked for her.

"Shut up," Gage demanded.

"Me or her?" asked the thief.

"Both of you."

Though Willow looked taken aback, she finally muttered, "Okay."

The sound of Gage releasing the hammers brought deadly silence.

Gage knew he had failed but refused to be the one who sent Willow to her death.

"Let her go, Hodge. Let's do this like men." He threw down the gauntlet. "Fist to fist."

"All right, lawman. Makes it easier on me. I ain't the one who can't see where I'm punching."

"Like I said, let her go first."

"You got a knife?" Hodge looked him in the eye as he moved the handle of the whip and uncoiled its length from around her. All that remained were the ropes that tied her feet and arms to the chair.

"You said it would be fist to fist," Willow reminded him.

"I also said *no talking*." Gage knew what game the thief played.

"If I remember right, you asked me to *shut up*. He's trying to make you put the gun down, Gage," Willow warned, "so your hands are busy with my ropes instead."

"I know, love. Don't worry." Gage nodded toward

the man who had confessed he didn't care to take on the corps. "You got a knife?"

The man shrugged. "Don't remember."

"Check. If you do, cut her loose. If not, then be very careful and dig into my left pocket and get mine."

"Got one." The fellow moved behind Willow's chair to cut her free.

She whimpered as the binds finally loosened and she could soothe the marks against her wrists. Her feet could barely keep her upright.

Gage's heart went out to her. He wanted nothing more than to grab her up into his arms and carry her into the house and never let her go. Instead, he said, "Now get out of here. Run if you can. Don't stop until you're far away from him."

"I'm not leaving you." She shook her head, setting her mop of curls free from the ribbon that had at one time held them back.

"You need to quit arguing with me for once and do what I ask."

"You can't handle your own woman, Ranger. What makes you think you can handle me?"

Willow turned and slapped her captor hard, leaving a handprint that jumbled his freckles together.

When Hodge lifted the handle of the whip to strike her, the fight was on.

Gage hurled himself at his foe. Willow kicked the whip out of the outlaw's reach. Fists connected with flesh and the crunching of bone echoed in the rafters. Blow after blow landed hard and deadly, stirring up dust as their feet scuffled and grunts echoed from somewhere deep inside the pain.

All of a sudden, a loop of rawhide hurled over Hodge, barely missing Gage. The man was yanked backward, fighting the rope Willow had managed to grab and throw dead center.

Gage got up from the ground, wiping blood from his lip, discovering the other men were long gone. He guessed they'd taken their leave when the leaving was good.

He stared at the pride in Willow's eyes as she tied off the knot that secured the horse thief to the same chair that had held her prisoner.

The sound of pounding hooves echoed the promise that Bear or the sheriff had finally arrived with the posse.

Ellie Finchmeister ran out of Daisy's house screaming, "I was kidnapped. You've got to believe me. Kidnapped, I tell you."

"A likely story." Gage laughed, opening his arms to Willow.

"One I'm sure she'll be telling for years to come," Willow said, stepping into his embrace.

"Thanks for rescuing me."

"Anytime," she promised.

He studied her face, knowing that as soon as it healed, he planned to ask her to marry him. If she didn't end up asking him first. He didn't care what she looked like, but Gage knew she did. He planned to treasure the beauty in how Willow felt about him.

"Do something for me, please?" she whispered.

"What's that, love?"

"Close your eyes and tell me what you see."

She wants me to dig deep. He smiled. "That you are what you hide unless you're willing to trust yourself to do better…even if it's just taking one step, or in your case, one good deed, at a time."

She nodded. "The finest deed *you* ever did was make me feel extraordinary. I can't thank you enough for that, Gage, and your words have set us free to love each other. Do you think you could ever be happy riding fictional trails with me, no matter how ordinary our real lives turn out to be?"

"There you go again, beating me to the punch. Shut up and kiss me."

And she did for the next fifty-two years and through dozens of Will Ketchum adventures.

* * * * *

Dear Reader,

Usually the author of the book writes a note to the readers, but in this case I'd like to do the honor.

In 1983, DeWanna Pace and I took a creative writing class at Amarillo College. We were both shy, just dreaming of writing and on opposite sides of a packed class.

But when she read, I almost screamed, "I want to write like her."

As soon as the class was over, we started meeting at the library, trading chapters every week. We shared knowledge and learned from each other. Five years later we were autographing books side by side. We traveled every weekend that first summer we both published.

Through births, deaths, illnesses and joy, we shared our dream of writing. We celebrated the ups and cried over the downs as we wrote at night, worked during the day and met every week to read.

I can still hear her telling me when I struggled, "How do you eat an elephant, kid?"

"One bite at a time," I'd answer through book after book.

We were always one another's best fan and true friend. So, though DeWanna Pace is Heaven's blessing now, I'd like to welcome you to step into one of her best stories from a long line of great books.

DeWanna made the real world a better place for living and left many novels that will continue to bring laughter and touch readers' hearts.

She'd be tickled to know others are enjoying this story.

Jodi Thomas

REQUEST YOUR FREE BOOKS!

2 FREE INSPIRATIONAL NOVELS
PLUS 2 *FREE* MYSTERY GIFTS

Love Inspired® H I S T O R I C A L

YES! Please send me 2 FREE Love Inspired® Historical novels and my 2 FREE mystery gifts (gifts are worth about $10). After receiving them, if I don't wish to receive any more books, I can return the shipping statement marked "cancel." If I don't cancel, I will receive 4 brand-new novels every month and be billed just $4.99 per book in the U.S. or $5.49 per book in Canada. That's a saving of at least 17% off the cover price. It's quite a bargain! Shipping and handling is just 50¢ per book in the U.S. and 75¢ per book in Canada.* I understand that accepting the 2 free books and gifts places me under no obligation to buy anything. I can always return a shipment and cancel at any time. Even if I never buy another book, the two free books and gifts are mine to keep forever.

102/302 IDN GH6Z

Name _____ (PLEASE PRINT) _____

Address _____ Apt. # _____

City _____ State/Prov. _____ Zip/Postal Code _____

Signature (if under 18, a parent or guardian must sign)

Mail to the **Reader Service:**
IN U.S.A.: P.O. Box 1867, Buffalo, NY 14240-1867
IN CANADA: P.O. Box 609, Fort Erie, Ontario L2A 5X3

Want to try two free books from another series?
Call 1-800-873-8635 or visit www.ReaderService.com.

* Terms and prices subject to change without notice. Prices do not include applicable taxes. Sales tax applicable in N.Y. Canadian residents will be charged applicable taxes. Offer not valid in Quebec. This offer is limited to one order per household. Not valid for current subscribers to Love Inspired Historical books. All orders subject to credit approval. Credit or debit balances in a customer's account(s) may be offset by any other outstanding balance owed by or to the customer. Please allow 4 to 6 weeks for delivery. Offer available while quantities last.

Your Privacy—The Reader Service is committed to protecting your privacy. Our Privacy Policy is available online at www.ReaderService.com or upon request from the Reader Service.

We make a portion of our mailing list available to reputable third parties that offer products we believe may interest you. If you prefer that we not exchange your name with third parties, or if you wish to clarify or modify your communication preferences, please visit us at www.ReaderService.com/consumerchoice or write to us at Reader Service Preference Service, P.O. Box 9062, Buffalo, NY 14240-9062. Include your complete name and address.